'So, you've
suspected,
time.'

At the sound of the voice from the steps behind her, the deep tones harsh and openly hostile, Liana spun round, startled, in her tracks.

She looked into the man's face. 'Who are you?' she demanded.

The man smiled a dark smile. 'I'm the one who sent the telegram.'

Dear Reader

Christmas is upon us once again, and with Christmas comes the thought of Christmas holidays, Christmas presents, and, of course, romance. This month's selection of books makes wonderful Christmas reading—you can drift away to the exotic Bahamas or imagine yourself having a romantic adventure in Argentina, or in the wilds of Mexico... Whatever your tastes, we know that we have a story that will be just right for you. May you all have a wonderfully romantic Christmas!

The Editor

Stephanie Howard was born and brought up in Dundee in Scotland, and educated at the London School of Economics. For ten years she worked as a journalist in London on a variety of women's magazines, among them *Woman's Own*, and was latterly editor of the now-defunct *Honey*. She has spent many years living and working abroad—in Italy, Malaysia, the Philippines and in the Middle East. Currently, she lives in Kent.

Recent titles by the same author:

A ROMAN MARRIAGE
UNCHAIN MY HEART
LOVE'S VENDETTA

DANGEROUS INHERITANCE

BY
STEPHANIE HOWARD

MILLS & BOON LIMITED
ETON HOUSE   18-24 PARADISE ROAD
RICHMOND   SURREY   TW9 1SR

All the characters in this book have no existence outside the imagination of the Author, and have no relation whatsoever to anyone bearing the same name or names. They are not even distantly inspired by any individual known or unknown to the Author, and all the incidents are pure invention.

All Rights Reserved. The text of this publication or any part thereof may not be reproduced or transmitted in any form or by any means, electronic or mechanical, including photocopying, recording, storage in an information retrieval system, or otherwise, without the written permission of the publisher.

This book is sold subject to the condition that it shall not, by way of trade or otherwise, be lent, resold, hired out or otherwise circulated without the prior consent of the publisher in any form of binding or cover other than that in which it is published and without a similar condition including this condition being imposed on the subsequent purchaser.

*First published in Great Britain 1992
by Mills & Boon Limited*

© Stephanie Howard 1992

*Australian copyright 1992
Philippine copyright 1992
This edition 1992*

ISBN 0 263 77834 7

*Set in Times Roman 11 on 12 pt.
01-9212-49006 C*

Made and printed in Great Britain

CHAPTER ONE

DROPPING her suitcase ahead of her on to the dusty roadside, Liana jumped down from the bus into the glare of the sun and paused to blink in amazement at the scene all around her.

'Are you sure,' she started to ask, 'that this is El Dotado?' This big rambling ranch house set amid acres of farmland, right in the heart of the Argentinian pampas, was light years away from what she'd been expecting.

But already the bus driver was revving up his engine and in a cloud of red dust was heading off down the road. This had better be the right place! Liana observed to herself wryly. There wasn't another bus out of here until tomorrow, she'd been told!

And then she caught sight of the big wooden sign nailed to the perimeter fence of the ranch house. 'El Dotado', it announced with reassuring simplicity. At least, after all, she was in the right place!

She picked up her suitcase and, shading her eyes with her hand, headed towards the big wide gate and the driveway that led up to the front of the house.

Inside her, her growing sense of bewilderment was edged now with a sudden sharp flicker of apprehension. Since her arrival in Buenos Aires early this morning, in response to an unsigned summons by telegram, she'd been subjected to one shock after another. What further shocks awaited her now?

The ranch house was surrounded by a wide wooden veranda that was approached by a flight of well-worn wooden stairs. Liana climbed them, hefting her suitcase behind her—in this ferocious heat, it seemed to weigh a ton!—and paused for a moment, gratefully, in the shade of the veranda, pushing back the damp strands of hair from her face.

The big front door of the ranch house faced her. Laying down her case and squaring her shoulders, she stepped towards it, knuckles raised to knock.

But her knuckles never quite made contact with the paintwork.

'So, you've arrived. As I suspected, you didn't waste any time.'

At the sound of a man's voice from the steps behind her, the deep tones harsh and openly hostile, Liana spun round, startled, in her tracks.

She looked into the man's face. 'Who are you?' she demanded.

The man smiled a dark smile. 'I'm the one who sent the telegram.'

He was in his middle thirties, Liana guessed, dressed in a pair of worn and faded jeans and a plain white T-shirt whose sleeves had been rolled back to reveal powerful biceps and a pair of deeply tanned shoulders. And although he was standing halfway down the wooden staircase, in a posture that was at once both relaxed and oddly menacing, the deep-set black eyes that looked back at her unblinkingly were almost on a level with her own. And their expression was as warm and friendly as a rattlesnake's.

He said in that same rough tone of before, 'You must have caught the very first plane available to have arrived here from London with such commendable speed?'

'I understood that was the intention of the telegram. To advise me that I should get here as quickly as possible?'

Liana's own tone, as she looked back at him, was equally hostile. Since the moment she had read that peremptorily worded telegram that had been delivered to her at her London flat just two days ago, she had decided that its sender was rude and overbearing. And now the living proof of that was standing right before her!

The black eyes never flickered. They seemed to lance right through her, two coal-black, sabre-sharp points of brightness in a face that was at once both harsh and deeply sensuous. This man, Liana sensed, would not employ half-measures. He would put his body and his soul into whatever he did.

And what he was doing now was, quite openly, studying her, the dark gaze moving over her face with its wide hazel eyes, high cheekbones and soft mouth framed in a shoulder-length fall of golden-brown hair.

He enquired, as his gaze now drifted a little lower to take in her petite and slender figure, dressed in white trousers and a simple pink blouse, both slightly rumpled from long hours of travelling, 'Are you always so quick to answer a summons? Do you always jump to it instantly whenever someone snaps their fingers?'

Liana did not answer for a moment. She was feeling physically exhausted after her long journey, and a little disorientated, a stranger alone in a strange country. Perhaps the man sensed that and saw her as vulnerable. An easy target for his rough manners.

But he was wrong about that. She was nobody's easy target! Feeling her fatigue transform itself into anger, with undisguised contempt she let her eyes scan his face.

'And are you always so damned uncivil?' she demanded. 'Is this the way you normally treat your guests?'

'You are no guest of mine.' He shot the words at her like bullets. Then he smiled a hostile smile. 'If you were, you would not be here.'

And what was that supposed to mean? Liana frowned inwardly. Then she narrowed her eyes at him and told him in an even tone, 'Look, the only reason I'm here is because I received your telegram telling me that Great-Aunt Gloria had died.' As she spoke the words, a sense of sadness touched her. She had never met Great-Aunt Gloria, but she had learned to love her through her letters. The news had come as a terrible shock.

She took a deep breath. 'The telegram also said that my presence was required here at El Dotado immediately. And that's why I'm here.' Her hazel eyes narrowed. 'For Great-Aunt Gloria's sake. To find out why I'm needed.'

'*Needed*?' A pair of jet-black eyebrows lifted. Straightening his tall frame, the arrogant stranger unhurriedly climbed the veranda steps, so that suddenly he was towering over her. 'Take my word for it, *señorita*, you are in no way needed. Please be in absolutely no doubt about that.'

His eyes fixed her for a moment, as cruel as rapiers. 'However, as I informed you in the telegram, your presence here is briefly required. A mere regrettable inconvenience, and one that I intend to dispose of swiftly.'

So saying, he swept past her almost roughly, the heels of his boots clicking sharply against the floorboards. He pushed the door open, shooting her a narrow glance across his shoulder. '*Very* quickly,' he elaborated as on long, arrogant strides he went into the darkened hallway.

Liana stood for a moment, glaring after him. No doubt she was expected to follow him indoors, though he hadn't even had the grace to invite her. Nor had he had the grace, she reflected, glancing down, to relieve her of the burden of her heavy suitcase. The man grew more abominable with every passing second!

Well, she could manage without his chivalry very well. And there was no way she would allow his rudeness to ruffle her. As Cliff was always telling her, she was one of life's copers. It would take more than this uncivil savage to upset her!

She grabbed her suitcase and stepped across the threshold into the deliciously air-conditioned interior. Then she deposited her suitcase beside a Spanish-style sideboard, elaborately carved, elegant and old-looking, closed the front door and glanced quickly around her. Where had he gone? He'd left her hanging here like a lemon!

Liana was about to call out, 'Where the devil are you?' when she was aware of a sound in one of the rooms off to her right. With a gasp of impatience she strode towards it, then stalled in surprise at the sight that met her eyes.

It was a beautiful room, full of brightness and light that spilled through the french windows that led out on to the veranda. And everything about it spelled opulence and comfort, from the big soft sofas, draped with brightly coloured rugs, to the huge gilt-framed paintings that adorned every wall.

And, again, it struck her that this was not what she'd been expecting. With every step she took she grew more puzzled.

She glanced at the tall figure who was crossing the room with what looked like an ice-cold can of beer in one hand. And there was impatience in her voice as, still standing in the doorway, she put to him, 'Don't you think it's time we introduced ourselves? Surely, that's the least we ought to do?'

'I already know who you are.' He had seated himself on one of the sofas. With a quick glance in her direction he yanked the ring pull from his beer can and tossed it neatly into an ashtray on the nearby coffee-table. 'You're Liana. Liana Bolton,' he elaborated. 'You're Tia Gloria's loving niece from London.'

There was a distinctly caustic edge to that last part of his pronouncement. He had spoken the word 'loving' as if it gave him a bad taste in his mouth. But, for the moment at least, Liana decided to let that pass.

She looked back at him with impatience, arms folded across her chest. He had said *'Tia'* Gloria, and *tia* was Spanish for aunt. Even with her scant knowledge of the language she knew that. 'And who,' she demanded in clipped tones, 'are you?'

'I told you. I'm the one who sent you the telegram.' He took a mouthful of his beer, then, without glancing at her, he waved towards the cabinet against the far wall. 'By the way, if you want a drink, the fridge-bar is over there. Don't stand on ceremony. Just help yourself.'

Don't stand on ceremony! That was a laugh!

'How very hospitable of you.' Her tone was laced with irony. 'I really am most deeply impressed.'

'Please don't be impressed. No hospitality was intended. I already told you you're not my guest.'

'That's right, you did.' Liana scowled across the room at him. What had she done to deserve all this antagonism? 'But what you still haven't told me is who you are.'

He took a mouthful of his beer. 'Who I am is a local farmer.'

'That's *what* you are, not *who* you are. I'd like to know your name and how you fit into all of this.'

'Would you, indeed?' He turned a sharp glance on her. 'I would say that, for a stranger, you want to know a lot.'

The dagger gaze fixed her for a moment, almost causing Liana to drop her eyes away. Then, annoyed at herself—that was just what he wanted, to intimidate her, to gain the upper hand!—she stepped very deliberately into the room, head held high, and confronted him.

'Look,' she bit at him, 'I've had a long day. I flew into Buenos Aires in the early hours of this morning after a sixteen-hour flight from London.' She glanced at her watch. 'It's now nearly four o'clock. I spent five hours on a bus getting from Buenos Aires to Trenque Lauquén, then I spent another couple of hours waiting for a bus to get me here and another couple of hours on the journey. I'm hot, I'm tired, I haven't eaten for ages, and I think I'm due a few explanations.'

'Do you?' The stranger took a mouthful of his beer and shot her a smile devoid of all sympathy. On the contrary, it struck Liana, he seemed to have derived a degree of satisfaction from her litany of misery.

He contemplated the beer can in his hand for a moment. Then, without glancing at her, he observed, 'Yes, I must confess, you have indeed gone to a great deal of trouble.' Then in a damning tone he added, 'You evidently consider your mission here to be of some importance.'

What was he getting at? Why this constant tone of condemnation? Whatever was behind it, it was time she put him straight.

'I have no mission here. At least, none that I'm aware of.' Liana had taken another step into the room and was now standing facing him across the coffee-table. Her tone was rough with her overflowing annoyance. 'I came because I received a telegram. "Great-Aunt Gloria died on Friday", it stated. "Your presence required at El Dotado immediately." You say you sent it, so you already know that.' Her voice rose. 'So, why did you send it and who the devil are you?'

He paused before answering and shook his head slowly. 'That was quite a performance. Almost convincing.' He slid her a look from beneath long black lashes. 'If you ask me, you're in the wrong profession. You ought to be on stage with a talent like that. It's really rather wasted on a journalist.'

'How did you know I was a journalist?' The cool revelation jolted her slightly. Who was this man? How did he know so much about her?

But, even as she was about to demand some answers, he laid down his beer can and rose to his feet. 'Since you are so eager to know my identity,' he told her, 'I shall do you the honour of introducing myself.'

Liana had assumed that he had risen to shake her hand. But no such politeness, quite clearly, had crossed his mind. He stepped right past her on long arrogant strides, heading for the fridge-bar in the cabinet against the wall, and helped himself to another can of beer.

Then he returned once more to the sofa where he had been sitting and reseated himself before continuing.

'I am, *señorita*, Felipe Mendez.'

'*You're* Felipe?' Liana's eyes widened. Surely not! she was thinking to herself.

'You seem surprised.' One black eyebrow lifted. 'For some reason this piece of news appears somewhat to have astonished you.'

Astonished was the right word. Liana frowned as she looked back at him. 'I confess I had expected Felipe to be rather different.'

'Different? In what way?' He smiled at her amusedly. 'How did you expect Felipe Mendez to be?'

For a start, she had expected him to be a gentleman. She had expected him to be courteous and civil and polite. She had expected him to be a man she could like and respect. Great-Aunt Gloria's occasional references in her letters to her beloved great-nephew, Felipe Mendez, had definitely given her that impression. It was little wonder she was astonished!

But she resisted the temptation to put her thoughts into words. He would not care in the slightest what she thought of him.

So she said instead, 'Perhaps I'm simply even more astonished than ever at your lack of hospitality. You are, after all, it would appear, my cousin.'

There was a silence as Felipe Mendez looked back at her. Then at last he said, 'Yes, that is indeed how it would appear.' It was perfectly clear that the thought of this relationship, this blood tie that existed between them, did not appeal to him in the slightest.

Neither did it appeal particularly to Liana. Yet it was undeniable. She told him plainly, 'My mother was your father's sister. Whether we like it or not, alas, that definitely makes us cousins.'

Felipe Mendez took a mouthful of his beer and sat back against the cushions of the sofa. He tilted back his head and regarded her through his lashes. 'You are wrong,' he told her, 'about one essential thing.'

'You mean you're not my cousin?'

'That was not what I meant.'

Pity, Liana thought. Such news would have cheered her.

She narrowed her eyes at him, 'So, what is it that I'm wrong about?'

'I have mentioned it before.' The dark eyes glinted. 'I am in no way beholden to offer you hospitality. So it is quite pointless your continuing to berate me for the lack of it.'

'I wasn't berating you. I was simply pointing out——'

'What? That my manners leave something to be desired?'

'You could say that.'

'I offered you a beer.' Felipe smiled with harsh amusement. 'What more do you want?'

Liana smiled sarcastically back at him. 'You told me where the beer was kept. In my book that's not quite the same thing as offering me one.'

'What should I have done? Fetched it for you and poured it for you?'

'That's what I would have done if you'd been a guest in my house.'

'But you are not my guest. This is not my house.'

'It's our aunt's house, and, since you know her better than I did and since you also, presumably, know the house well, it wouldn't have killed you to have been a bit more——'

Liana had been about to say 'hospitable' again. She stopped herself short, overcome with frustration. What the devil was she doing, arguing such inanities with this infuriating man who didn't give a damn anyway? Had she just travelled virtually halfway across the world to waste time in this sort of idiotic conversation?

She shook herself inwardly. It was time she took control. She had been letting him mess her around for long enough!

Folding her arms across her chest, Liana took another step towards him. 'Why did you wire and tell me that my presence was required? I presume there was a good reason why you wanted me here?'

'Oh, yes, there was a good reason.' Felipe contemplated her for a moment, letting those black, insolent eyes of his travel unhurriedly over her, as though examining her in intimate detail.

Liana felt herself shift uncomfortably beneath his scrutiny. His eyes seemed to caress her, sensuously, yet contemptuously, as though they could reach beneath the rumpled cotton of her blouse and trousers to the warm, living flesh that pulsed beneath.

Then he smiled a small smile and raised his eyes to meet hers again. 'I'm a little surprised you made the journey alone. I had expected that your fiancé, Cliff, would accompany you.'

At the mention of Cliff's name Liana felt an automatic warmth. Dear Cliff. What would he make of this uncivil savage?

But she refused to allow Felipe to divert her. She reminded him, 'You haven't answered my question.'

'He's a tax adviser or something, isn't he?' It was as though she had not spoken. 'Wasn't he able to take time off?'

Liana took a deep breath. She felt like hitting him. How dared this rude, uncouth individual have the nerve to quiz her about her fiancé? A man, she thought fondly, who was worth a dozen of him!

She glared at Felipe as he continued to watch her. He was well aware of, she sensed, and was thoroughly enjoying the intensity with which he angered her.

In measured tones she put to him, 'Will you answer my question? Will you tell me why you demanded my presence here at El Dotado?'

The black eyes never flickered as he took a mouthful of his beer. Like the evil eyes of Satan they remained fixed on her face.

'It's a long way for a girl to come on her own. As I said before, you must really have been keen.'

With a gasp of impatience, Liana swung away from him. In just another moment she would grab hold of him and throttle him. Breathing slowly to calm her anger, she crossed to the fridge-bar. A cool beer at this moment might not be a bad idea!

Keeping her back to Felipe, she extracted a can, took down one of the tall glasses from a nearby shelf and observed over her shoulder, as she poured the cool pale liquid, 'There are plenty of glasses here, if you'd like one?'

'If I'd wanted one, I would have taken one.' His tone was mocking. 'Do my manners bother you, *señorita*?'

Liana smiled to herself as, still with her back to him, she took a long, slow mouthful of her beer, feeling its welcome coldness course down her gullet.

She had drunk many times straight from a can herself. It wasn't that that bothered her. It was the man himself. The offer of a glass had simply been intended to annoy him.

She turned now to face him. 'Something's going on. Something that I appear to be in the dark about. All those innuendoes you keep making... As though you believe I had some ulterior motive for coming here...' She looked Felipe in the eye. 'Perhaps you wouldn't mind explaining?'

Felipe smiled, but it was not a smile of amusement. 'You really are a damned fine actress,' he shot at her. 'What made you choose journalism instead of a career on the stage?'

Liana felt her fingers tighten around her glass. She took a mouthful of the beer to douse the rage within her. Then, deliberately avoiding that infuriating dark gaze, she walked calmly towards the armchair opposite him.

'I can see this is going to take some time.' Her tone was heavily loaded with sarcasm. She flicked him a quick glance. 'I hope you don't mind if I sit down?'

'Not in the slightest. And even if I did...' He paused and looked across at her steadily. 'It isn't really my place to object.'

That sounded uncharacteristically self-effacing. As Liana lowered herself against the comfortable cushions, she couldn't quite suppress a cynical smile. Felipe Mendez was the type of man who would consider it his place to do anything he wished!

So absorbed was she with this thought that she almost missed his next remark.

'After all, when it comes down to it, the chair is yours.'

There was a moment's silence. Liana frowned across at him. 'What do you mean the chair is mine?' Then she smiled a little tentatively as an explanation occurred to her. 'Do you mean that Great-Aunt Gloria left this chair to me in her will?'

Felipe nodded. 'Yes, as a matter of fact she did.' He smiled a cold smile. 'Does that please you?'

'Very much. It's a beautiful chair!' In surprised delight Liana swivelled round to admire the handsome tapestry-covered chair.

What a lovely thing for Great-Aunt Gloria to have done, to have left her a small memento of their friendship! The gesture touched her to the heart.

'She also left you this sofa I'm sitting on. And that other chair over there. And the one by the window.'

There was a bite in his voice that made Liana look across at him, bewildered, abruptly abandoning her admiration of her new chair.

'In fact,' he continued, 'she left you every chair in the room. Every chair in this house, to be more precise.'

He was leading up to something. Liana sat very still, aware of a sudden nervous tick in her throat.

'What do you mean she left me all the chairs in this house?' She felt suddenly as though a bomb was about to explode in her face.

'I mean what I say, my dear *señorita*. Tia Gloria has been most generous to you. Not only has she left you all the chairs in the house, she has left you every single stick of furniture. Not to mention, of course, also the carpets and the paintings... In fact, she has left you the entire contents of the house...'

Liana's jaw had dropped open. She could not believe what she was hearing.

'...and, just in case you have nowhere to put them, she has most thoughtfully also left you the house as well.'

'This house?' Surely he must be joking?

But there was no hint of humour in the dark eyes that flayed her. 'Yes, *señorita*, this house belongs to you now. As indeed do also five thousand acres of the most fertile land in Argentina.'

Felipe sprang to his feet, as though he could no longer contain his emotions. And the black eyes were fierce, his hands clenched as he flung at her,

'Don't look so surprised! Stop acting the innocent! I happen to know you planned this very carefully. What you are is a cheat and a thief, *señorita*!'

'I don't know what you're talking about!' Liana's head was spinning. 'I'm not a thief. I didn't plan anything!' She could scarcely think straight. It was all too much to take in.

With an angry gesture Felipe swept aside her protestations and took a step towards her, bristling with anger. 'But what you didn't realise when you plotted this little coup is that, before you lay a hand on your cleverly acquired inheritance, I'm afraid you'll have to contend with me!'

He scowled down at her like thunder. 'And there you made a big mistake. It was not wise of you to pick me for your enemy!'

CHAPTER TWO

LIANA stared into Felipe's outraged face in shattered silence for a moment. The only sound she was aware of, in the aftermath of his angry outburst, was the sudden astounded gallop of her heart. What on earth, she was thinking dully, had she got herself into?

He had turned away from her sharply, as though he could not bear to look at her, and stood now facing the tall french windows. The broad powerful shoulders beneath the thin white T-shirt were stiff with barely controlled emotion.

Liana addressed the broad back, sitting forward in her seat, her tone as even as she could manage.

'I suspect you're not going to believe this,' she told him, 'but I really don't know what you're talking about. All these accusations of secret plots and plans don't even begin to make any sense to me.'

Felipe did not respond. He continued to stare out of the window.

Liana carried on, still in that measured tone, 'The only reason I came here was because of your telegram. I had no idea about... anything else...'

At that last part her voice trailed off disbelievingly. Could it be true what he had told her about her inheritance? Did she really own this house and all these acres of land?

'You had no idea?' His tone was rough. He did not look at her.

'No idea at all. How on earth could I have? I didn't even know that Great-Aunt Gloria owned all this! She never told me in her letters. I had no idea she was a wealthy woman!'

His response was a cynical shake of the head. He flashed her a hard look over his shoulder. 'No, of course you didn't!' he taunted.

'I didn't! Really, I didn't!' Is that was he was thinking, that she'd devised some kind of plot to benefit financially from her great-aunt Gloria's death?

The notion was offensive, but it was also ludicrous. Liana shook her head dismissively. 'If only you knew! I had imagined that Great-Aunt Gloria lived in some cosy little suburb in a modest little bungalow called El Dotado!'

She half smiled to herself, remembering her astonishment when at Buenos Aires airport she had hailed a taxi and asked the driver to take her to El Dotado. The man had been honest and, before she climbed inside his taxi cab, he had quoted her a price that had made her jaw drop. 'It's over six hundred kilometres, *señorita*,' he had informed her. That was when she had decided she'd better take a bus!

Then had followed the rest of her astonishing journey away from the city of Buenos Aires, across the vast tract of land that bore the same name, till at last she had arrived, dazed and weary, two long bus rides later, at the ranch house.

'I was absolutely flabbergasted when I arrived here!' she assured Felipe.

'I'll bet you were.' His tone was rough metal. At last he swung round in his tracks to face her. 'I expect it was all even better than you'd hoped.'

'I'd *hoped* for nothing!' Liana sprang to her feet in anger. His insinuations were outrageous! 'You have no right—and no reason—to accuse me of such a thing!'

'Wrong on both counts.' Felipe took a step towards her. 'I have every right, and plenty of reasons, to accuse you of being a gold-digger, *señorita*.'

All at once he was standing very close to her, so close that she could smell the warm sun on his skin and feel, without touching it, the silky blackness of his hair. Something stirred within her. A sense of sudden danger. It took all of her will-power to resist stepping away.

She looked into the black eyes, feeling the power behind them, and sensed again what she had sensed at first sight of him—that he was a man who would pursue his passions and his convictions wholeheartedly, with single-mindedness and vigour.

And he had been right, he was not the man to choose as one's enemy.

In a firm voice she told him, 'I am not a gold-digger.'

He smiled a cynical smile. 'No? Then what would you call yourself? What name would you give to a clever young woman who deliberately manipulates a dying old woman into making her the main beneficiary of her will?'

Liana was stunned for an instant. Her hazel eyes narrowed. 'Dying? What do you mean dying?' she demanded. 'I knew that Great-Aunt Gloria was old, but I had no idea that she was dying.'

'Just as you had no idea that she was wealthy?' The dark eyes swept her face, openly disbelieving. 'What a perfectly innocent little creature you are!'

'What an actress!' was what he meant. 'What an unprincipled liar!' The message shone like a beacon from every line of his face.

Liana drew herself up tall. 'You're totally wrong about me. When I say I had no idea about Great-Aunt Gloria's circumstances, and certainly no idea that she was dying, it may sound unbelievably innocent, but I swear to you it's the truth.'

'You mean you didn't know that for the past two years Tia Gloria was bedbound, that she was dying of heart disease?'

'I didn't know, I tell you! She never mentioned it in her letters! She never even gave me the smallest hint!'

'And she never mentioned the ranch or the house or anything? She never indicated that she was one of the wealthiest women in the region?'

'None of that! I swear to you, not one word of it! I never got the impression that she was destitute, but I assumed she was a woman of moderate means!'

'Moderate means! How carefully you express yourself! I can see that you've rehearsed your part to perfection!' With a snort of impatience, Felipe swung away angrily, snatched his beer can from the coffee-table and drained its contents.

Then he swung back again to glare at Liana. 'But even, *señorita*, if what you say were true, that she mentioned none of these things in her letters, you would have known about Tia Gloria from your mother. Your mother was born and raised here. She, at least, must have told you that Tia Gloria's means were rather more than moderate!'

Your mother. Your mother. The words spun in her head. And the sudden sense of grief that reared up inside her was so huge and so intense that it took Liana's breath away.

Tears pricked her eyes. She glanced away quickly and breathed deeply in an effort to contain the pain that filled her.

She heard herself say in a voice that echoed strangely, 'My mother never told me anything about Great-Aunt Gloria.'

He had picked up her reaction. His eyes were on her. He told her in a flat tone, 'I was sorry about your mother's death.'

They were only words, with no real value. Liana knew that, but still she could not reject them. She nodded in acknowledgement. 'Thank you,' she murmured. Since her mother's death just over a year ago she had gathered to herself gratefully every word of comfort offered her. Each one had helped her to cope with the immensity of her loss.

And she had coped. She had been strong enough, though it had not been easy. And if she could cope with that, with the sudden death of her beloved mother, then there was nothing in the world she could not cope with.

She raised her eyes to Felipe's, once more in control of herself. 'My mother told me nothing about Great-Aunt Gloria. I knew she existed, but that was all I knew. It was only after the accident...' Her voice trembled. 'After my mother's death... when she sent a note of condolence, that I started corresponding with Great-Aunt Gloria. But, as I told you, she mentioned neither her money nor her illness in her letters.'

Felipe continued to watch her, his black eyes unreadable. Then he took a step back and reseated himself on the sofa. 'I find it hard to believe that your mother told you nothing.'

Did he? 'That's your problem,' Liana told him candidly. 'It doesn't in any way alter the truth.'

As she looked back at him she was aware of a sense of relief that he had increased the physical distance between them, and that he had seated himself and no longer stood towering over her. His closeness, his physical dominance, she had found oddly disturbing.

She hovered for a moment, wondering if she should also reseat herself. But for the moment she decided to stay where she was. She rather enjoyed looking down on him for a change!

He was leaning back against the cushions of the sofa, his hair dark and glossy in a shaft of bright sunlight. And it suddenly struck Liana that he was quite extraordinarily good-looking. Too bad he had the temperament of a pit bull terrier!

He seemed unaware of her scrutiny. Dark eyes unblinking, he stretched his long legs out in front of him. 'No,' he agreed. 'Nothing can alter the truth.'

There was a silence as, for a moment, each surveyed the other. There were so many things Liana wanted to know—about the house, about the ranch, about Great-Aunt Gloria—but Felipe was definitely the wrong one to ask. Whatever she said to him, he was bound to twist it and change it to make it fit this unfortunate ugly image he had of her.

But there was one thing she wanted to know. 'Did Great-Aunt Gloria die peacefully? Did she die in hospital or here at home?'

'She died in her own bed, just as she had prayed to do.' There was something very still about him as he said it. 'I was with her. Her passing was mercifully peaceful.'

Liana nodded, feeling grateful for this assurance. She felt glad the old lady had not died alone.

But her train of thought was broken as Felipe fixed her with a look. 'That was quite a correspondence you carried on with Tia Gloria. A letter a week. You really made an effort.'

It had not been an effort. It had been spontaneous and enjoyable. The letters to and fro had flowed quite naturally.

But Liana did not say so. Let him keep his cynicism. Instead, she observed, 'You seem to know a lot. Did Great-Aunt Gloria tell you that we were writing to one another?'

'She mentioned it.' He crossed his long legs at the ankles, the toes of his boots pointing at the ceiling. 'But I had no idea of the frequency of the correspondence until I discovered your letters the other day.'

A bell rang in her head. Suddenly Liana sensed she knew where he had discovered all those little bits of information about her. What she did for a living, that she was engaged to be married, that her fiancé was a tax adviser in the City.

She looked back at him accusingly. 'You read my letters! I really don't think you had any right to do that!'

Felipe looked back at her, unrepentant. 'What are you so worried about? Are you afraid I might have discovered all your secrets?'

'I'm not afraid of anything! I have no secrets to be ashamed of! I just happen to think your curiosity is in rather poor taste.'

'Do you?'

'Yes, I do!'

'That's very interesting. Well, allow me to tell you what *I* think is in poor taste, since we appear to be exchanging opinions.' He sat forward in his seat and impaled her with a look. 'What I personally believe to be in very poor taste is the way you cynically exploited Tia Gloria, buttering her up with all those false words of affection, telling her how close you suddenly felt to her, promising her that you would come and visit her soon.'

'I intended to visit her!'

'Yes, after she was dead and buried! You couldn't make the effort while she was alive, but you dropped everything and got on the first plane available when it was time to pick up your inheritance!'

It was a vicious accusation. For a moment it stunned her. There was no truth in it all. It was sheer fabricated malice. For one fleeting moment Liana could not answer him.

Then she pulled herself together. 'You have no right to say that. No right at all! I was planning to visit her! Cliff was going to come with me! We were planning to come next Easter.'

'A little late, don't you think?' Felipe's tone was crushed granite. 'The most optimistic medical prognosis only gave her till the end of last August. She was already living on borrowed time.'

'But I didn't know that! If I'd known, I'd have come sooner! I wanted to meet her—more than you can know!'

'I'll bet!' Felipe made an angry gesture of impatience. 'I suppose that's why you've waited twenty-four years?' He paused. 'I am right, am I not? It is twenty-four years? Never once in your entire lifetime, in spite of how desperately you wanted to, did you take the trouble to visit the old lady.'

'I had no contact with her until my mother died! It's not fair! You're accusing me of things I'm just not guilty of! If I had known she was ill, I would have come immediately. I wasn't interested in any inheritance. It was my aunt I cared about!'

She might have saved her breath. He was not interested in her protestations. That was obvious from the dark look that bored into her now. He had made up his mind about her and that was final.

With a sigh of frustration, Liana sank down in her chair. Why was she bothering to defend herself, anyway? Let him believe what he liked. It didn't matter a damn to her.

She glared across at him. He was a hateful individual. And then a thought struck her. She narrowed her eyes at him. 'About those letters that you took it upon yourself to read... The ones I wrote to Great-Aunt Gloria...'

'The ones that so clearly reveal your intention to trick a childless old widow into leaving everything to you...?'

Liana pointedly ignored that. 'As I was saying... Those letters happened to be private...'

'They were not yours any more. They were the property of Tia Gloria.'

'And *my* property now, since the house belongs to me. You had absolutely no right to read them!'

'Perhaps you also believe I have no right to be sitting on this sofa?' It seemed to Liana, as he said it, that he leaned more firmly against the cushions. His eyes sparked a challenge. 'Or even to be in this house? Perhaps it is your wish to personally eject me?'

That thought had crossed her mind. In fact, it appealed to her quite strongly. But Liana smiled and responded, 'I wouldn't dream of it. You see, I have a naturally hospitable nature.'

He smiled back at her then, a real smile that surprised her. For there was something compelling about the force of that smile. It possessed a warmth and a passion that stirred her strangely.

'That's a relief.' He was still smiling as he said it. 'To be physically ejected by a young woman like yourself could prove a slightly embarrassing, if interesting, experience.'

He was mocking her, of course. Liana was well aware of that. No one, least of all a fragile girl like herself, would be capable of ejecting Felipe Mendez from anywhere from which he did not wish to be ejected.

Yet, extraordinarily, she was aware of the tiniest *frisson*. Behind the mockery she had sensed a hint of something else. A quite inappropriate hint of sexual challenge.

And it was inappropriate, both the challenge and her response to it. The man was her cousin, she was engaged to be married, and in every respect she found him unbearable!

Sternly, she informed him, 'Hospitality is one thing, but reading someone's private correspondence is something else.' She delivered what she hoped was a look of crushing disapproval. 'I consider that, as I told you, to be in very poor taste.'

'Especially when the contents of the correspondence in question reflect you in a somewhat dubious light.'

Her disapproval, far from crushing him, simply ran off him. He leaned back against the cushions and stretched his arms along the sofa back, a gesture at once both arrogant and eloquently composed. And his arms, deeply tanned and powerfully muscled, she had to confess, were a masculine work of art.

She snatched her gaze away. 'That's your interpretation. For some reason it seems to fit your prejudices about me.' She sat back and looked at him, laying her hands along the chair arms. 'But that doesn't alter the fact that you had no business reading those letters.'

'I'm afraid you're wrong about that.' His arms flexed subtly. She caught the ripple of hard muscles beneath the sun-bronzed flesh. 'I had every right in the world to read them.'

'Why? Because you were her great-nephew?'

'I didn't say that.'

'Then what are you saying?' She shook her head impatiently and added before he could answer, 'This house, so you've just told me, belongs to me now. This house and everything that's in it. It appears to me that you had no right at all.'

The dark eyes surveyed her. 'Don't get greedy. To say that *everything* belongs to you is not strictly accurate...'

He paused just long enough to force her blush to deepen. She was not being greedy. Greed did not enter into it. But the way he had looked at her had made her feel guilty. A quite unwarranted blush of embarrassment had touched her cheeks.

She said, almost apologetically, 'I thought that was what you told me.'

'If I did, the error was mine, *señorita*. The house, the furniture, the carpets, the paintings... Even the forks and spoons and the pans in the kitchen, even the linen in the cupboards and all the books on the bookshelves... All of these things, thanks to your dedicated and affectionate correspondence, now legally, if not rightfully, belong to you...'

He paused and raised an admonitory finger, and wagged it at her, a gesture that annoyed her. 'But the letters, I'm afraid to say, do not. Tia Gloria left all her private papers to me.'

'I see.'

'I'm glad to hear it. So you will now understand that I was well within my rights when I read those letters?'

Liana delivered him a narrow look. She could not dispute that. But she was wondering, none the less, why he should have *wanted* to read her letters.

Almost certainly out of malice, she decided, saying nothing. Everything he did concerning her appeared to be motivated by malice.

She crossed her legs in their slim white trousers and addressed him in a businesslike tone. 'I think it would be a good idea if I was to get in touch with Great-Aunt Gloria's solicitor and obtain written details of the situation. It would be helpful if I could know exactly what is and what is not mine.'

'By all means.' Felipe was watching her with that insolent black look of his. 'But it's really very simple. The house and all its contents—minus private papers—along with the land and the outhouses within the boundaries of the ranch house...all of these are now your property. And of course five thousand acres of prime arable land.'

Liana shook her head as bewilderment once more overtook her. 'It's extraordinary,' she murmured, really to herself. 'Why on earth would Great-Aunt Gloria leave the house and the ranch to me?'

'Half of the ranch.'

Liana snapped her eyes up. 'I beg your pardon? What did you say?'

'I said *half* of the ranch.' Felipe smiled coldly. 'The other half she left to me.'

'Oh?' Liana blinked at him. Her mouth turned down at the corners. This revelation, she knew instinctively, did not bode well.

'The ranch, in all, covers ten thousand acres. Five thousand are now yours and five thousand are mine.'

'I see.'

'So, we're partners.'

'How unfortunate.'

Felipe nodded slowly. 'My feelings precisely. I can think of no arrangement that could possibly be less satisfactory.'

'I'm sure you can't.'

'Take my word for it. It was not a good idea to divide the ranch between the two of us.'

Liana looked into his face and suddenly she understood what lay behind all his hostility and his malice. It was very simple. He had accused her of greed, but he was the one who was guilty of that sin.

She should have tumbled to it sooner. The reason he hated her was because he had been hoping to inherit everything himself!

As she absorbed this obvious truth, Liana suddenly experienced her first real sense of pleasure at her windfall. It gave her a feeling of immense satisfaction to know that she'd knocked his odious nose out of joint!

Unable to resist a smile as she said it, she put to him with just a touch of facetiousness, 'I think the best idea would be if we were just to divide it down the middle. Then we can each, quite independently, attend to our own half.'

Felipe smiled without amusement. 'A quaint solution. And I must confess it has its charms. But that option is excluded to us by the terms of the will. The ranch must remain intact, exactly as it is. Inconvenient as it surely is, we now jointly own the whole.'

Inconvenient, Liana decided, was far too mild a word. The thought of any joint enterprise with this hateful man ranked high in her hierarchy of most hideous prospects.

But even as she looked at him, silently but eloquently expressing this thought through her deep hazel eyes, Felipe was leaning forward, elbows on thighs, with the sort of smile that, she sensed, spelled trouble.

'There was another point stipulated in the will, besides the one about keeping the ranch intact...'

Hiding a twinge of apprehension, Liana continued to look back at him. There was no need to ask what. He was obviously dying to tell her.

'Tia Gloria was most emphatic about one thing... The terms of the will only continue to stand if the two beneficiaries—that's me and you—take an active part in the running of the ranch.' He smiled and informed her, digressing for a moment, 'By the way, that's what I was doing here—fulfilling my responsibilities, not waiting to welcome you...'

Then he continued his explanations regarding the will. 'If, after a period of six months, either one of us can prove that the other has not been pulling his or her weight, then the share of the inheritance of the defaulter will automatically accrue to the other party.'

He smiled with relish. 'In other words, *señorita*, in six months' time this ranch house we're sitting in, its contents and your five thousand acres, will, as they ought to have done anyway, pass to me. And you'll be left without a penny.'

That prospect really appealed to him. She'd been right, he wanted all of it. Liana looked back at him steadily. 'Don't be so sure.'

'Oh, but I am sure.' He stood up suddenly and looked down on her with arrogant black eyes. 'All your manipulations will have come to nothing. You won't even have gained the cost of your postage stamps.'

Liana rose to her feet slowly, squaring her shoulders as she did so. 'Oh, no,' she said softly, 'I won't let you get your hands on it.'

'And how will you stop me?' He tossed his dark head at her. 'In a few days' time you'll be back in London. You can't take an active part in running the ranch from there.'

He turned on his heel. 'Have a nice holiday. Spend it looking around your temporary inheritance and see what a splendid windfall has slipped through your fingers.'

'It hasn't slipped through my fingers.'

'Oh, but it will. You have my guarantee.'

'And you have my guarantee that it won't.'

He tossed her a harsh look over his shoulder. 'In six months all of this will be mine.'

As he strode through the doorway, Liana glared after him. He was wrong. He would never get his hands on her inheritance.

I shall hang on to every stick and stone of it. And that's a promise, she vowed in silence.

How she planned to do it she hadn't a clue. But she would do it somehow. She would find a way. Never would she grant Felipe Mendez the satisfaction of taking over what was hers!

CHAPTER THREE

NEXT day Liana discovered that that promise she had made herself, more than likely, would prove impossible to keep. It would take a miracle to stop Felipe getting his hands on her inheritance.

For he had been absolutely right about that condition in the will. In order for Liana's inheritance to stand, she was required to take an active part in the running of the ranch. And he had been equally right about what the consequences would be were she to fail to meet that condition. The house and her share of the ranch would pass to him.

Liana had just spent the last couple of hours, in the privacy of his office in Trenque Lauquén, with the distinguished Señor Pedro Carreño, Great-Aunt Gloria's lawyer and the executor of her will.

He had explained everything to Liana about the terms of the will, and most of it had been pretty depressing.

'On the face of it I can see no way that you can hang on to your inheritance. For it's clearly impossible for you to take an active part in running the ranch from the other side of the Atlantic.' Then he had paused for a moment and added in a cautious tone, 'Unless we can find a way round that condition.'

'Do you think that's possible?' Liana had instantly brightened.

'It may be.' The distinguished grey head nodded. 'Though, of course, at this stage, I can't promise anything.'

'Don't worry about promises. Just try,' she'd exhorted him. 'Just do your best. That's all I ask.'

She stepped out of his office now into the broiling midday sunshine, her brain buzzing with all the things she had learned during their meeting. For she had learned more than just the facts about her inheritance. Carreño had also, during the course of their conversation, unwittingly supplied certain information that had explained a great deal about Felipe Mendez.

Now she knew for sure what was at the root of his hostility to her. And she felt deeply shocked by the lawyer's inadvertent revelation of what a shameless, unprincipled villain Felipe was.

But before she dwelt on that, there was something she had to do first. As quickly as possible she must find somewhere to eat! She hadn't eaten a bite since breakfast at seven-thirty and the pangs of hunger were gnawing like rats at her insides!

Liana glanced around her quickly, scanning the busy street, trying to recall where she had noticed on her way into town a promising-looking *confiteria*. And then she spied it, across the road, on a corner. She smiled to herself. It looked like just what she needed!

Jabbing on her sunglasses against the glare of the sun, Liana waited for a pause in the noisy stream of traffic and hurried across the dusty road, heading for the *confiteria*.

She had noticed several of these little places—they were like a cross between a restaurant and a snack bar—but El Matador, as this one was called, had a particularly tempting array of foodstuffs in the window.

Liana stepped gratefully into the fan-cooled interior and was shown to an empty table in a corner. As the waiter handed her a menu, she tried out her phrase-book Spanish. '*Un zumo de naranja,*' she told him. '*Y una comida corrida, por favor.*'

What she had just requested was a glass of orange juice and the fixed-price set lunch of the day. That, she decided, might be easier than trying to decipher the menu!

She sat back in her seat with a sense of satisfaction, in spite of the gloom the lawyer had heaped on her head. If the odious Felipe could see her now!

'You'll never make it on your own. You'll get lost,' he'd assured her in that arrogant way he had, as though he knew everything. 'As inconvenient as it will be, I'll take you to see the lawyer.'

After that dramatic exit, when he had stormed out of the sitting-room, threatening that he intended to swallow up her inheritance, he had thankfully disappeared from her sight for a while. Then, about half an hour later, when she had been through in the bedroom, unpacking her suitcase and hanging her things in the wardrobe, he had suddenly appeared, unannounced, in the doorway.

'I wouldn't bother going to all that trouble, if I were you, stowing your things away so neatly. It seems like a great deal of unnecessary bother, considering how brief your stay here's going to be.'

Liana threw him a sharp look. 'It's no trouble,' she assured him, pointedly continuing what she was doing. 'I wouldn't dream of leaving my things all crushed up in a suitcase. Some of us like to look presentable.'

As she said it she turned briefly, her gaze pointedly scanning his worn, shabby jeans and far-from-new-looking T-shirt, rolled back casually to his shoulders. Unlike you, her eyes told him as she delivered this small insult—it was high time he was given a taste of his own medicine!—I have no wish to look like a vagabond!

Felipe smiled back at her uncaringly. 'It still seems pointless to me. In a couple of days' time, they'll all be going back in the suitcase.'

Liana turned away from him and did not answer. He was correct in his assumption that she was not planning on staying long. It was her intention to stay for a week at the most. But all the same she found it deeply annoying that Felipe should have the cheek to spell out her itinerary!

With her back to him, continuing to hang her skirts and dresses in the wardrobe, she said, 'I'd like you to give me the name of Great-Aunt Gloria's lawyer. I want to arrange to meet him as soon as possible.'

'I think you ought to. He has some papers for you to sign.' Liana could feel the dark eyes on her as he added, 'I'll take you to him tomorrow morning.'

Liana glanced round then. 'That won't be necessary. Just give me his name and telephone number. I'm quite capable of making the arrangements myself.'

'His name is Pedro Carreño. I don't have his number on me, but I can very easily get it for you.'

He paused as Liana felt her eyes widen in astonishment at this uncharacteristic display of cooperation. She had been expecting to have to beat the information out of him! Then with a smile he added, as though he had read her mind, 'Not that his phone number will be a great deal of use to you. I'm afraid there's no phone at El Dotado.'

'No phone?' Momentarily, Liana forgot about Carreño. Damn! she was thinking. How inconvenient. She'd been planning to phone Cliff as soon as she'd unpacked, just to let him know that she'd arrived safely.

Felipe was smiling, enjoying her dismay. 'The old lady refused to have phones installed. One of her little eccentricities. So, as I said, Carreño's phone number wouldn't really be much use to you.'

Liana wrenched her thoughts from her fiancé back to Carreño. 'Then just give me his address. I'll go personally to make an appointment.'

Felipe shook his head. 'No, *señorita*. It is better that you come with me.'

Liana levelled a hard look at him. 'If you don't mind, I'll find my own way.'

'That might be rather difficult.'

'Why? Where do I have to go?'

'Carreño's office is in Trenque Lauquén, about a hundred kilometres from here.'

A hundred kilometres. Was that all it was? On the overcrowded bus that had brought her from Trenque Lauquén on the second leg of her journey from Buenos Aires, stopping at every little village on the way, it had felt as though it were at least twice that distance! And though she didn't exactly relish the thought of repeating that journey tomorrow, Liana relished even less the thought of Felipe's accompanying her.

She told him, 'That's no problem. I'll take the bus.' And I'll phone Cliff from Trenque Lauquén, she added to herself, feeling relieved that a solution to that particular problem had been found.

'And stay overnight at Trenque Lauquén? Would that not be a little inconvenient? You see, there's no bus back until the following day.' Felipe leaned with arrogant amusement against the door-jamb. 'I really think you ought to accept my offer.'

There could be only one reason why he was making his kind offer. And it was not even remotely, Liana was well aware, out of anything akin to concern for her convenience. What he was contriving was that she should conclude her business here quickly, head back to London and leave the ranch to him. Then he could start ticking off the six months on his calendar—the six months at the end of which he hoped to take over her inheritance.

But he was wrong if he thought she was about to fall in with his plans. 'There must be some other way of getting there?' she insisted.

'You tell me.' He shrugged broad shoulders as he continued to stand there in the doorway. He was enjoying her dilemma. He was an odious man.

'A car? What about a car? Is there a car I could borrow?'

'There's certainly a car—though you would have no need to borrow it. It's yours. It's in the garage. It goes with the house.'

'Then that's what I'll do.' Liana smiled with satisfaction. Fortunately, she had had the foresight to bring her international driving licence. 'There, I knew there was bound to be a perfectly straightforward solution!'

'I think it would be more straightforward if you were to allow me to accompany you. You don't know the road. You'll get lost. I guarantee it.'

'Then I'll get one of the ranch hands to come with me. One of them must surely know the way?'

'I'm sure all of them do... but none of them can be spared.' Felipe threw her a black implacable look. 'You either come with me or you don't go at all.'

The black eyes and the hazel eyes met and clashed. You could almost hear the reverberations ringing around the room. Then they held for a moment. A look passed between them. And again Liana was aware of that quick pulse of danger and of an almost visceral flare inside her. The air all around them all at once was electric.

Liana tore her eyes away and turned her back on him, hastily resuming her unpacking. 'That's where you're wrong,' she said quietly, but decisively. 'I'll go on my own.' She'd had enough of his bullying!

But then she started and swung round again as with a sudden brusque movement Felipe stepped into the room to stand glowering down at her.

'You'll do nothing of the sort, *señorita*!' he told her harshly. 'You may think it very clever to go off on your own—perhaps that kind of foolish gesture appeals to you. But I'm afraid I forbid it. You see, it would not appeal to me to waste hours out on the pampas looking for you when you get lost!'

There had been, until that moment, just the tiniest seed of doubt in Liana's mind at the prospect of making the journey alone. But that seed of doubt had now been crushed to oblivion.

Who did he think he was talking to? 'I forbid it', indeed! There was no way in the world he was going to tell her what to do!

But before she could speak her mind, he was swinging away from her. 'We'll discuss it no further. I'll pick you up at nine tomorrow morning. Be sure you're ready. I don't like to be kept waiting.'

And with that he had departed. A moment or two later, Liana had heard his car rev then crunch off down the drive. Oh, boy, had he underestimated her! she was thinking. There was no way she was going to let him get away with this!

She smiled to herself now as she sat at the corner table in the little *confiteria* in Trenque Lauquén, sipping the orange juice the waiter had brought her. Felipe's arrogant veto had simply spurred her into action!

The first thing she had done was to check out the car—which was in the garage, just as Felipe had told her. A white Mitsubishi Shogun, obviously well maintained, it had, as she quickly discovered, a full tank of petrol and a set of keys handily stowed in the glove box.

When it had started first time, its engine as clean as a whistle, Liana had grinned triumphantly. She was halfway there!

There were some road maps stowed in one of the door pockets of the Shogun. Liana had hurried back indoors with them and studied them with growing excitement. The route to Trenque Lauquén was actually pretty simple. Felipe must have a very poor opinion of female drivers if he seriously thought she'd have any trouble getting there!

But there still remained one vital problem. She had to track down the lawyer's address!

As the waiter appeared now with her starter, a dish of piping-hot *empanadas*—a kind of pasty stuffed with cheese and vegetables—Liana reflected on her original decision just to come to Trenque Lauquén, even without Carreño's address, and somehow track him down once she was here. She was a journalist, after all! She was good at that sort of thing!

But, in the event, such drastic measures had not proved necessary.

It had been after Felipe had gone yesterday evening, just as she'd finished showering and changing into her cotton bathrobe with the intention of fixing herself something to eat, that she'd become aware that someone was tapping on the front door.

She'd known before she answered it that it wasn't Felipe. Felipe was incapable of making such a discreet, polite sound. Any knock of his would loosen the door from its hinges, if indeed he bothered to knock at all!

'*Soy Rosaria, señorita!*' a woman's voice had called to her as she hesitated a moment, wondering whether she should open up or not.

Liana had pulled the door open and found herself looking into the kindly bright-eyed face of a darkhaired young woman. The woman had held out to her the bundle she was carrying in her arms—a cooking pot, steaming hot, wrapped in a tea-towel. It looked as though Liana's supper had arrived!

Half an hour later, after a great deal of laughter, and with the aid of a Spanish-English dictionary, Liana had discovered who Rosaria was. The wife of one of the ranch hands, she had cooked and cleaned for Great-Aunt Gloria, and was, she had insisted, eager to do likewise for Liana.

Liana was perfectly capable of cooking and cleaning for herself, but she'd sensed that the modest sum Rosaria demanded for her services probably meant a great deal to the woman. So she agreed. 'OK.' Then she had explained very carefully that the position would be temporary and very, very brief.

'*Gracias. Gracias. No importa.*' That doesn't matter, Rosaria had assured her, adding quickly that she would be delighted to assist her new employer in any way she could.

And that was when the idea had come to Liana. Perhaps Rosaria knew Great-Aunt Gloria's lawyer's address!

At first Rosaria had shaken her head when Liana put the question to her. '*No se.*' I don't know, she'd answered, frowning. Then, as she thought about it for a moment, her face had lit up. '*Esta cerca del oficina de correos!*'

Liana had rifled through her dictionary, checking she had understood. Then her own face had lit up. She'd given Rosaria a hug. Carreño's office was near the post office! That shouldn't be too hard to find!

Rosaria had insisted on spending the night at the ranch house, instructions, Liana suspected with just a flicker of annoyance, that had more than likely come from Felipe, who was also no doubt responsible for the woman's arrival on her doorstep! Perhaps, it had even occurred to her, Rosaria, however innocently, had been planted to keep an eye on her. Felipe would be perfectly capable of using people in that way.

But whether or not Rosaria's presence had been imposed on her by Felipe, Liana had felt quite grateful for her company. The house was big and strange and in the middle of nowhere. It was nice to know there was someone else sleeping under the same roof.

She'd lain in bed for a while, thinking of Cliff. Dear Cliff, the warm safe bedrock of her life. The man she loved. The man she would marry. He'd be worried, she knew, that she hadn't yet called him and the thought of his anxiety filled her with dismay. Tomorrow she would phone him and set his mind at rest.

She'd smiled to herself, thinking of all the things she had to tell him—about her journey here, about her amazing inheritance, about her clash with the abominable Felipe Mendez. Though of the latter she would be sparing in her details. Cliff, always so thoughtful and protective of her, would be horrified if he knew how rudely Felipe had treated her!

She had pushed that thought away and snuggled deeper beneath the covers. The thought of Cliff was soothing. The thought of Felipe was definitely not!

Peacefully, thinking of Cliff, she had drifted into sleep.

And now the phone call to Cliff was the only task left to complete. Liana had resisted the temptation to phone him this morning immediately on her arrival in Trenque Lauquén—after a dusty one-

and-a-half-hour drive, during which she hadn't got lost once! It had been just after nine-thirty local time, but back in London Cliff would still be fast asleep! She would call him, she had decided, at a more civilised hour.

According to Señor Carreño, Great-Aunt Gloria's lawyer, with whom she had just spent a most informative couple of hours, the ENTEL office, from which she could make an international phone call, would now be closed for lunch until two o'clock.

That suited Liana fine. By then in London it would be nine a.m., and she would be sure of catching Cliff at the office.

She finished her *empanadas*, sat back in her seat and took another mouthful of her orange juice. As it turned out, it was better that she had spoken to Carreño first before getting in touch with her fiancé. As a result of that meeting, there was something she had to discuss with Cliff. As a result of that meeting, an idea was forming in her head.

But Liana got no further with these thoughts.

At that very moment, just as the waiter was stepping towards her to clear away her plate and bring her her main course, Liana froze in her seat, blinking in disbelief.

Were her eyes deceiving her? Was it actually possible that the tall dark figure who had just come bursting through the doorway, like a whirlwind, sweeping aside all in his path, was actually who she believed it to be—the current bane of her life?

Her eyes were not deceiving her. It was Felipe, all right. In a couple of strides he had swept past the waiter, almost causing the poor man to drop his tray in fright, and was standing before Liana, eyes burning with fury.

'So, there you are!'

'Yes, here I am.'

'You look pleased with yourself. Perhaps you're thinking I ought to congratulate you?'

'Not in the slightest.' Was she really looking pleased with herself? Liana had rather imagined she must be looking startled. The way he had come storming up to her she had been half expecting that he would sweep the table to one side and grab her by the scruff of the neck!

But, instead, with a display of quite amazing self-control—*he* was the one who deserved to be congratulated!—he was pulling out one of the wooden chairs opposite her and, to Liana's dismay, lowering his tall frame on to it.

'I suppose you thought you were being very clever, playing your silly little games?'

His tone was low, controlled. Liana responded similarly.

'Clever? Not at all. The journey was perfectly easy.' Her eyes flashed with subdued pleasure as she deliberately misunderstood him. 'And I haven't been playing any little games,' she added. 'If I had, I most certainly wouldn't have been playing them with you.'

He did not smile exactly, but something flickered in his eyes. Liana wondered if she ought not to have said that last part. He seemed to have read something into it that had not been intended.

Then his gaze grew hard again, as he leaned back in his seat and looked at her. 'I told you I was coming to pick you up at nine o'clock. Don't try to tell me you had forgotten that small detail?'

'And I told you that I would take the car and drive in myself. Or have you forgotten *that* small detail?'

As his eyes narrowed, Liana was half expecting that he would remind her that he had 'forbidden' her to make the journey by herself. If he did, she would waste not a moment in informing him that nobody, but nobody, forbade her to do anything. Only the law and her own conscience had such power. And most certainly not Felipe Mendez!

Perhaps he could read that message in her eyes, for he did not take it upon himself to remind her. Instead, with one of his stock of arrogant gestures, he signalled to the waiter, who was still hovering near by, to proceed with what he had been about to do, namely serve Liana her main course.

'*Y traemi una cerveza y un bife de costilla. Muy jugoso, por favor,*' he commanded the waiter as the poor man hurried away.

Liana watched him disapprovingly from beneath her lashes. He was dressed today a little less shabbily than yesterday, in a pair of light-coloured trousers and a blue check shirt—no doubt in honour of his anticipated encounter with Carreño.

That must have cost him quite an effort, Liana thought to herself with a sense of satisfaction that his effort had been so resoundingly wasted!

Having finished with the waiter, Felipe turned once more to Liana and continued as though there had been no break in their dialogue, 'You had no business taking the car and going off on your own.' The black eyes bored into her over the table.

'Why not? The car is mine and I have a perfectly valid driving licence.' And, what's more, I'm fully insured, she added silently. That small detail she had learned with relief from Carreño. 'I can't see what was stopping me going off in it if I wanted to.'

'That is not what I meant.' His tone was impatient. 'We had an arrangement, and as a result of you breaking the arrangement I have just been obliged to waste nearly two hours driving here and another one searching every street in this town for you.'

He had no idea how much that pleased her. 'You needn't have bothered. I was managing very well.'

'And how was I supposed to know that? Am I suddenly supposed to be telepathic?'

Liana resisted the urge to express her surprise that telepathy was not among the gifts to which he laid claim. Such reticence, from a man like Felipe Mendez, amounted almost to a show of modesty.

She shot him a hard look. 'Why was it necessary for you to know? I am not, I hasten to assure you, any responsibility of yours.'

'Perhaps I think you are.' His eyes raked her countenance. 'You are, after all, a niece of Tia Gloria. And you are a stranger and alone in this country. In my eyes that throws a certain weight of responsibility on to my shoulders.'

'I'm afraid I don't agree.' Liana sat back in her chair. She had noticed that deft piece of verbal footwork, that careful reference to her as a 'niece of Tia Gloria'. Quite clearly he found the idea of referring to her as his cousin equally as distasteful as she did.

But that was the only point upon which they were agreed! She continued, 'I am in no way, shape or form your responsibility. The only person whose responsibility I am is my own. And take my word for it, I'm quite accomplished at looking after myself.'

The waiter had brought the beer Felipe had ordered. Felipe took a mouthful. 'Heroic words.' He leaned back in his seat and let his eyes travel over her. 'No doubt what you say is not without truth. You have the look of a young woman who is, if I may say so, most able and accomplished in many areas...'

As he paused, eyes still on her, bold and appraising, the warm touch of a blush brought a glow to Liana's cheeks. She sat back in her seat, putting some distance between them. That remark, with its impudently sexual overtones, had suddenly caused her to be aware of how they must appear to the other diners—like two squabbling lovers, hissing at one another across the table.

That picture simultaneously disturbed and appalled her. She said in a voice that was cool and controlled, 'I repeat, I'm very good at looking after myself.'

'No doubt in your own environment you are. But this is Argentina. We are in the middle of the pampas. We are not, *señorita*, in Hampstead Garden Suburb!'

'I'm quite well aware of that!'

'Then act as though you were!'

'Don't tell me how to act! I know how to act! I made the journey here in a perfectly responsible manner!' She was leaning towards him again. And she was hissing.

Liana sat back abruptly, and switched back to cool and controlled. Why did it always require such an effort, she thought crossly, to behave in a detached manner with this man? He seemed forever to be drawing her emotions to the surface.

'I had maps,' she continued. 'I had plenty of water and I also had a full tank of petrol. I wouldn't have been so stupid as to set out otherwise. But in your book I suppose I owe you an apology for denying you the satisfaction of finding me lying face-down in some ditch.'

Liana caught the flicker of amusement that touched his lips, though there was little of it reflected in his tone as he shot back at her, 'That would have given me no satisfaction, I assure you. That would simply have been yet one more inconvenience to add to all the others that you have inflicted on me.'

The waiter chose that moment to bring the rest of his order. *Bife de costilla, muy jugosa*, Liana could now see, was T-bone steak done extremely rare.

That figured, she thought angrily. He would enjoy the sight of blood. That was why he was goading and tormenting her. But he would not make her bleed. His hostility would not wound her. He could continue to goad and torment all he liked!

As if to demonstrate this fact, she grabbed her fork and knife and sliced off a piece of the meat roll on her plate. It was delicious, she discovered as she popped it in her mouth. The stuffing was of spinach and egg and onion. She smiled her enjoyment of it defiantly into his face and couldn't resist informing him, 'This is absolutely mouthwatering. Definitely not the kind of thing they serve in Hampstead Garden Suburb.'

Felipe's response was a scowl of dark humour. He dug into his steak as he looked across at her. 'In that case, enjoy it while you can. After all, you won't be having many more opportunities. In a few days' time you'll be back in London.'

Liana snatched her gaze away as something flared inside her. His words had sounded almost like a challenge. With a kind of instinctive defiance, she had felt herself respond.

And all at once the idea that had been forming in her mind before he had so rudely come bursting in on her seemed to fill her brain. She could feel it take firm shape.

She laid down her fork and glanced quickly at her watch. 'That reminds me...' She let her eyes drift back to Felipe's. 'When I've finished my lunch I have to find the ENTEL office. I have a telephone call to make to London.'

'I shall accompany you.' Felipe smiled across at her. 'It will be my pleasure. No doubt the purpose of your call is to inform your fiancé of your imminent return?'

Again that flare inside her. Liana held his eyes. 'Accompany me if you wish. But I'm afraid I must warn you...' She paused, questioning the wisdom of what she was about to say, yet knowing that nothing in the world now could stop her.

'The purpose of my phone call is not, as you suggested, to inform my fiancé of my imminent return...'

As he watched her, she continued, 'On the contrary, I'm phoning for quite the opposite reason... To tell him that I'll be staying on at El Dotado until I can find a way to secure my inheritance...'

She smiled with enjoyment as he regarded her stonily across the table. 'In order to fight you, I've decided to stay on. Indefinitely!'

CHAPTER FOUR

LIANA had been fully expecting some imperious response. That Felipe demand that she reconsider. Some kind of veiled threat. She was almost disappointed when, instead, he simply nodded. 'I see,' he murmured, without even looking at her.

The man was totally unpredictable, she decided, watching as he proceeded to demolish his *bife de costilla*, while she finished her *matambre arollado*. And she had no previous experience with unpredictable men. Cliff was the opposite. Cliff was safe and reassuring.

And that was how she liked her men. Safe and reassuring. This unpredictable savage seated opposite her she found deeply unsettling in a way she could not quite fathom. When she was around him her senses seemed to be constantly on alert. She felt unable to relax, unaccountably tense. He seemed to threaten her in a way she could not put a name to.

Though she could scarcely have faulted his behaviour for the rest of the meal. They chatted politely about nothing in particular over ice-cream and a couple of cups of black coffee, then they left the restaurant and, without a word of dissent, Felipe accompanied her to make her phone call, waiting discreetly out of earshot while she spoke to Cliff.

Then he observed, 'If you have no more business in town, I suggest we start heading back to El Dotado.'

'We?' Liana didn't much care for that 'we'. 'I'm quite capable of finding my own way back. You go ahead if you're in a hurry.'

'I think you should come, too.' A flicker of impatience. 'It'll be starting to get dark in a couple of hours or so. I know you made the journey here without mishap, but I wouldn't fancy your chances so much in the dark.'

Neither, now that she thought about it, would Liana. It irked her, but she realised he was talking sense.

She shrugged reluctantly. 'OK,' she conceded. 'I'll come back with you. I'd finished my business anyway.'

'I'll drive in front and you can follow behind.' His eyes fastened with hers. An ironic smile touched his lips. 'Or we can do it the other way around, if you prefer?'

Liana pulled a face. 'You lead, I'll follow.' Point taken, she told him with her eyes. You find claims to female equality amusing. 'After all,' she conceded practically, 'you know the road better than I do.'

As she drove along behind him on the homeward journey through the astonishingly beautiful scenery of the pampas, she couldn't help wondering what awaited her at El Dotado.

Did this calm façade of his disguise an inferno? Was he really still boiling with rage inside? Perhaps he was simply waiting until they were alone together before grabbing her by the throat and exploding with fury?

It made no difference, Liana reflected. He would not intimidate her into reversing her decision. Having spoken to Cliff, she felt even surer of that. Cliff, despite the fact that he was clearly disappointed that she would not be returning home immediately, had given her his full and unconditional support.

'If that's what you feel you ought to do, darling,' he had told her when she had explained her change of plan, 'you go right ahead and do it. You're the best judge of the situation.'

'I won't stay a moment longer than I need to.' At the sound of his voice, affection and warmth had flooded through her. He was a man in a million. He never failed to support her. 'I'll be back in London just as soon as I can,' she had promised him. For, in spite of her threat to Felipe to stay on 'indefinitely', she was keen to wind things up as quickly as possible.

Cliff had laughed and reminded her, 'Enjoy the sunshine while you can. It's freezing cold here. One of the coldest Januaries on record. Weather-wise, at least, you're better off where you are.'

Then on a more sober note, he had added, 'If you have any problems, be sure to let me know immediately. If that cousin of yours makes trouble for you, promise you'll let me know at once?'

'I promise,' she had assured him. 'But don't worry, I'll be all right. He's an absolute pig, but I don't think he's actually dangerous!'

As she kept her eyes fixed now on the bumper of Felipe's Range Rover, she crossed her fingers and hoped she was right! According to the signpost they had passed just a few moments ago, El Dotado was only a couple of kilometres along the road. One way or the other, she was about to find out!

Sure enough, at the very next bend in the road, the Range Rover turned off into the driveway of El Dotado. Liana felt her stomach clench a little nervously. What was about to happen now? she wondered. Was she about to see the volcano erupt?

They drew up, side by side, outside the ranch house. As Liana climbed out of the Shogun, Felipe spoke to her.

'I could do with a drink. If you have no objections, I wouldn't mind sampling that hospitality of yours.'

Well, she'd set herself up for that one! Resignedly, Liana nodded. One corner of her had actually been daring to hope that he might just turn around and go back to wherever his home was.

She told him, 'Sure, if you're thirsty, come in. I suppose the least I can do, after all the inconvenience I've put you to, is offer you a glass of cold beer.'

'I'd agree with that.' He smiled inscrutably. 'And, besides, I think we ought to have a little chat.'

Liana said nothing as she turned and headed for the front door. Her supposition had been right. He preferred to dismember her in private!

But a surprise awaited her as she stepped into the hall. From out of nowhere a smiling Rosaria appeared.

'*Señor. Señorita.*'

The woman greeted them both warmly. Then she said something in Spanish to which Felipe responded, '*Muy buen. Gracias,*' before turning to Liana with one of those amused dark smiles of his and explaining, 'In your honour, we're to be served English tea in the drawing-room. I must say, that sounds extremely civilised.'

Liana felt herself relax. With Rosaria present, he was more likely to keep his anger under control. Though she had to confess, as she met his eyes momentarily, that he did not seem in the slightest put out by this development. It even occurred to her, as she headed towards the drawing-room, that he had known all along that Rosaria would be here. Perhaps it had never been his intention to dismember her, after all!

Without waiting to be invited, he had seated himself on the sofa, stretching out his legs and crossing them at the ankles. Liana slid him a look of open displeasure—how did he always manage to look as though this were *his* house? He ignored her look totally as he observed, 'So, how was your meeting with Carreño? Did he tell you all you needed to know?'

Liana seated herself in the armchair opposite the sofa, leaned back comfortably and told him, 'My meeting with Señor Carreño was most satisfactory.'

'Good. I'm pleased. But I must confess to some surprise.' Felipe paused and lifted one straight black eyebrow. 'If Carreño explained about the inheritance—in effect repeating what I'd already told you—I can see no sense to your decision to stay on here.'

Liana looked straight back at him. 'I can't think why you say that. I've already told you the reason why I'm staying.'

'In order to take steps to secure your inheritance?' He smiled. 'But, *señorita*, that is not possible. Unless, of course, you intend to stay on here permanently?'

What a ridiculous notion! Liana waved it aside. 'I intend to stay on until a way can be found.' In her mind, and in her conversation with Cliff, she had set a limit of two or three weeks. Surely some solution could be worked out by then? It *had* to be. She couldn't afford to stay on forever!

He seemed to read her mind. 'What about your work? It would be unwise of you to neglect your journalistic career in pursuit of a goal that cannot be achieved.'

'Don't worry, I shall see to it that my career doesn't suffer.' She meant that. Her thriving career was important to her. 'You see, I work as a freelance for several different magazines. And I have no outstanding commissions at the moment.'

She stopped short her explanations. He was not the least bit interested. All he was interested in was getting his hands on her five thousand acres!

'You could gather material for an article on Argentina while you're here,' Felipe observed, seeming to contradict what she'd been thinking. Then he added with an unmistakable touch of venom, 'You may as well not entirely waste your time.'

That was more like it! Liana tilted her chin at him. 'I may just do that—gather material for an article. But, more importantly, as I said, I shall take steps to secure my inheritance.'

'It can't be done.'

'That's what you say.'

'Did Carreño tell you differently? If he did, he was misleading you. There is no way round that condition of Tia Gloria's.'

'You sound very certain.' Liana was evasive. Carreño, after all, had simply said that it was possible that there *might* be a way. And she didn't intend revealing that to Felipe!

She flicked Felipe a diminishing glance. 'I didn't realise you were a lawyer.' She said it as though there might actually be some doubt. 'I had no idea you were an expert in such matters.'

He simply smiled at her mockery. 'I am no lawyer, *señorita*. I'm afraid I have far too honest a disposition for so devious a profession.'

That was genuinely funny. Liana burst out laughing, and Felipe at least had the grace to laugh with her. For a moment, as his eyes twinkled, a spark of something passed between them.

'However,' he was continuing, still smiling amusedly, 'one does not need to be a lawyer to know that you are embarked on a wild-goose chase.' He shrugged. 'In the end, there can only be one outcome. Carreño, after he has charged you a great deal of money, will simply confirm what I'm telling you now, and you will regret not having taken my word for it in the first place.'

'I shall never regret that.' Liana tossed him a bold smile. 'The only thing I would have regretted was if I'd failed to stand up to you.'

'You enjoy a good fight, do you?' The black eyes danced as he challenged her. 'That is good. I, too, enjoy a good fight.'

Liana was aware of a warm flush touching her cheeks. Confrontation was not something she normally sought out, but to her surprise she realised Felipe was right. She was rather looking forward to this particular fight. There was something quite stimulating, even exciting, about the flashing verbal swordplay between the two of them. It was a new experience. It made her blood rush.

Liana stopped that thought short. Suddenly it made her feel uncomfortable. She was confusing excitement with simple adrenalin-charged antagonism. Antagonism, not stimulation, was what this was all about.

Felipe was smiling. 'So, go ahead and fight. Waste your time and your money, if that's what you want.'

Liana met his gaze scornfully. 'I intend to waste neither. Both, I can assure you, will be put to good and productive use.'

'Namely to ensure that I don't get my hands on your land—the spoils of deception that you have worked so hard for?' Felipe laughed a mocking laugh. 'We shall see, *señorita*.'

At that precise moment Rosaria appeared, pushing a trolley laden with tea things. A silver teapot, cream and sugar, and an eye-stopping array of dishes piled high with sandwiches and muffins and fresh cream cakes.

Instantly, Felipe was rising to his feet, murmuring an appreciative '*Maravilloso!*' as he proceeded to make space on the low mahogany coffee-table that stood in front of the sofa where he had been seated. In response a delighted Rosaria beamed from ear to ear.

Liana watched the scene with a sense of bemused irritation. How brilliant he was at putting on a show. He could turn on the charm like turning on a tap! Here he was, masquerading as the perfect gentleman, and somehow carrying it off with effortless panache, as though such perfect manners came to him quite naturally, as though he were incapable of behaving in any other way.

But then he had this quality, Liana acknowledged grudgingly, this inner poise which, added to his physical presence, imbued him with a power that was both compelling and seductive. What a pity that he used that power so selfishly, as a mere tool to gratify his ambitions and his greed.

No doubt he had really turned on the charm with Great-Aunt Gloria, it occurred to her, remembering what Carreño had told her. And no wonder the poor woman had been taken in!

As Rosaria departed, they helped themselves to tea and a couple of wafer-thin cucumber sandwiches. Liana bit into hers and regarded Felipe. She would enjoy letting him know what she had learned about him.

She sat back in her armchair and observed conversationally, 'Señor Carreño was telling me about Great-Aunt Gloria.'

'Oh, really?' Felipe stirred his tea without looking at her. 'And what was he telling you? Anything interesting?'

Liana chewed slowly and took a mouthful of her tea. Shocking would be a more appropriate word than interesting. She laid down her teacup. But she would come to that in a moment.

'He told me about El Dotado, about how Great-Aunt Gloria and her husband built it up from nothing.'

'Indeed they did. When they bought the land forty years ago, it was totally uncultivated. Nothing grew here.'

'And now it's one of the most productive farms in the area.'

'And one of the most profitable.' Felipe smiled cynically. 'That, of course, is something you were not aware of previously.'

'No, I wasn't. As I've already told you, I didn't even know the farm existed until I got here.'

Felipe snapped his fingers in a parody of remembering. 'That's right. I'd forgotten. It all came as a huge shock.'

'Yes, it did.' Liana looked back at him, her gaze cool and steady. 'But you knew, didn't you?' Her tone was full of accusation. 'You knew precisely what every acre was worth?'

'Within a few centavos.' At least he did not deny it. He leaned back against the cushions of the sofa, his dark head wreathed in the light from the window, and regarded her down the length of his arrogant, shapely nose. 'And what particular significance do you draw from this fact?'

Liana simply looked at him. She would answer that in a moment. But, in the meantime, let him wait and wonder. For once, she was the one with her hand on the tiller!

Popping the remains of her sandwich into her mouth, she chewed in silence for a moment. Then she observed conversationally, 'Señor Carreño told me that, after her husband died ten years ago, Great-Aunt Gloria continued to run the ranch single-handed. That was quite a task for a woman of her age.'

'She had help.'

'You mean the ranch hands?'

'Yes, I mean the ranch hands.'

'But she did all the accounts, made all the decisions. That must have been a pretty stressful workload.'

'She was a very able woman, and dedicated to El Dotado. She loved the work. I never heard her complaining.'

Liana allowed a moment of silence to tick by. She reached for another sandwich and looked him in the eye. Inadvertently, he had provided her with the perfect opening. Now she would tell him what was on her mind.

She smiled a sweet smile. 'That's hardly surprising. After all, you weren't around to hear her complaining.'

'Meaning?'

Liana shrugged. 'Meaning precisely what I said. Correct me if I'm wrong, but I understand from Señor Carreño that you never set foot on El Dotado during those ten years that she was left alone.' She took a bite of her sandwich and narrowed her eyes at him. 'That is, until she suddenly fell ill and was given only a couple of years to live.' Her gaze hardened as she surveyed him. 'Do you deny that?'

He did not answer immediately. The dark gaze seemed to flicker. Then he said very quietly, 'No, I do not deny it.'

'At which point,' Liana continued, 'when you discovered she was dying, you suddenly, propitiously, turned up on her doorstep and proceeded to make yourself indispensable...'

Liana tossed down her sandwich. Suddenly she could not swallow. Her outrage had lodged like a stone in her throat.

'You accused *me* of self-seeking manipulation, but *you're* the one who should have a guilty conscience! The way you behaved was despicable!' she spat at him.

Her heart was hammering inside her. Outrage and anger poured helplessly through her. It was shaming to think that this monster of a man bore the same family name that had once belonged to her dear mother!

Felipe appeared quite untroubled by her attack on him. Unhurriedly, he helped himself to a mouthful of his tea. Then he put to her in a mocking tone, 'And what ought I to have done? According to you, would it have been less despicable if I had continued to allow her to fend for herself?'

Liana glared at him. 'Of course not! That's not what I'm suggesting!'

'But, surely, if I had done that, you would not now be accusing me of this self-seeking manipulation that is supposedly ravaging my conscience?'

'Ravaging your conscience?' Liana laughed a mocking laugh. 'I strongly suspect you have no conscience!'

To her annoyance, he smiled. 'Perhaps you are right. That would certainly explain why it is failing to bother me.'

Liana looked back at him. She found his attitude faintly shocking. Such hardness, such lack of caring, was barely human.

In a tone that made no effort to disguise her feelings, she told him plainly, 'If you had been a half-decent nephew, you would have visited Great-Aunt Gloria and taken an interest in the ranch after her husband died—or even before that—and not waited like a vulture till she was virtually on her deathbed.'

'Like you, you mean? At least be honest. Surely there were two vultures waiting by her bedside?'

'No, only one. I wasn't out to gain anything. As I already told you, I didn't know she was dying, and nor did I know that she was a woman of some wealth.'

Felipe shook his head, but he did not argue. There was no need. His disbelief was written plainly on his face.

He reached for a muffin, bit into it and chewed thoughtfully. 'So, what is basically troubling you,' he put to her, watching her, 'is that because of my despicable behaviour, because of my self-seeking manipulation, I do not deserve to inherit El Dotado. Not even the half that is already in my possession, and most certainly not the entire ten thousand acres, which of course will be the case when in due course I take over your share.'

He paused. 'Am I correct? Does that sum up the situation?'

Liana nodded. 'More or less, though I feel obliged to remind you that you will never take over my five thousand acres.' She delivered him a harsh look. 'You see,' she elaborated, 'I have a very strong dislike of people who use people.'

It was the strength of that feeling that had planted in her mind the notion that perhaps she should stay on and fight him.

Earlier on, it had actually crossed her mind that it really might not be such a bad thing if her share of the ranch was to pass to Felipe. At least he knew how to run it and, as hateful as he was, it might even be the case that he deserved to inherit it.

But as soon as she had learned from Señor Carreño that Felipe's association with Great-Aunt Gloria and El Dotado dated only from the time when the old lady had been virtually bedridden, she had angrily rejected that fond notion. He had already profited far more than he deserved from the cynically contrived couple of years' work he had put in, and she was perfectly prepared to use every means at her disposal to stop him profiting even more.

The fact that he was evidently so desperate to do so simply added to her determination!

She watched him polish off the muffin and reach for another one. Then he looked her in the eye and asked a question. 'So, we've established that you consider me an undeserving heir...' He smiled a humourless smile as he bit into the muffin. 'Perhaps now you would be good enough to enlighten me as to why you consider yourself to be so deserving?

'After all,' he pointed out, as Liana hesitated an instant, 'even if somewhat belatedly, I did play a useful part in Tia Gloria's life. You, if I may remind you, never even met her.'

That momentary hesitation had been due to honest deliberation. This was not the first time it had crossed Liana's mind to wonder what had possessed Great-Aunt Gloria to leave her house and half her land to a great-niece she'd never met, who was based in London and who knew as much about ranching as a cat knew about playing the piano.

So far she had come up with only two explanations. The first was straightforward. She offered it to Felipe. 'I think it's possible that over the year we corresponded Great-Aunt Gloria grew to be quite fond of me. I know I became extremely fond of her. We forged a friendship. There was a lot of warmth between us.'

She sat back in her seat and crossed her legs at the ankles. 'I'm not suggesting for one moment that I therefore *deserve* to inherit anything. But I think Great-Aunt Gloria's appreciation of our friendship may have been partly what motivated her to make the gesture.'

Felipe looked back at her, his dark eyes shuttered. 'As I mentioned before, *your* letters were indeed affectionate. Quite extraordinarily so, if I may say so.'

'They reflected my feelings.'

Her tone was clipped as she answered him. Liana had no intention whatsoever of elaborating any further on that statement. He would never understand how much it had meant to her to make contact, soon after the tragic death of her mother, with someone who had known her mother as a child. The friendship had sprung from there, from a shared affection for her dead mother, but very quickly had turned into something more personal, something that was warm and special in its own right.

She felt a sudden flash of anger that Felipe should question that. And it was that anger that triggered her next remark.

'However,' she pointed out, looking him straight in the eye as she said it, 'I also believe it's possible that Great-Aunt Gloria may have had an entirely different reason for including me in her will.'

'I was just about to ask you that. You hinted you had another theory.' With no great display of interest in her imminent revelation, Felipe sat back against the sofa cushions and chewed on his muffin.

Liana decided to be merciless. No beating about the bush. She would give it to him straight between the eyes.

She regarded him candidly. 'I think it's perfectly clear. Great-Aunt Gloria, after all, was far from being an idiot...'

'She was very far from being an idiot. She was an extremely smart woman.'

'As I was saying...'

That interjection had not been necessary. Perhaps he had guessed at what she was about to say to him and was trying to put her off her stride.

He seemed to confirm that theory now by smiling across at her and inviting her in an arrogant tone, 'Please carry on.'

Liana straightened in her chair and narrowed her eyes at him. 'As I was saying, it is my belief, since we appear to be in agreement that Great-Aunt Gloria was far from stupid, that before she died she tumbled to what you were up to and decided to scupper your greedy little plan to end up with El Dotado in your pocket.'

There was a momentary silence. Felipe swallowed his muffin. 'An interesting theory. Who knows? There could be something in it.'

'I believe there could be.' Did nothing flap him? She could throw anything at him and he would not bat an eyelid. 'So, you see,' she elaborated, her tone edged with annoyance, 'if that was the case, I'd be letting Great-Aunt Gloria down if I was to allow you to take over my half of the ranch.'

He actually smiled that amused, arrogant smile of his. 'That would never do. That would be most irresponsible. I can see now that it is no less than your duty to oppose me.'

She had thought that, just for a moment, she had her hands on the reins, that, briefly, it was her turn to be in charge of the situation. But somehow, effortlessly, he had snatched that power from her. It seemed she could not make a move that he could not instantly better.

Liana looked into his face with its strong hard lines and suddenly sensed that he knew precisely what she'd been thinking.

He proceeded to prove her right as he leaned back against the cushions. 'I can see from your puzzled look that you can't quite make me out. Do you find that frustrating, *señorita*?'

'Frustrating? No.' It was maddening, that was all.

He smiled. 'I, too, have not quite figured you out.' He caught her eyes and held them. 'Figuring one another out could prove to be a most diverting experience.'

'I doubt it.' Liana snatched her eyes away, but not before the look in his had caused her heart to shift strangely. That look in his eyes, a look of promises and mysteries, had stirred something forbidden and secret inside her.

As she shook the feeling from her, Felipe spoke again, with typical unpredictability changing the subject completely. 'Did Carreño tell you about the letter?'

'The letter?' For one moment Liana looked back at him blankly. Then she remembered. Just before she had left his office, the lawyer had shown her a plain white envelope.

'Your aunt also left you this,' Carreño had told her. 'I have no idea what it contains, but her instructions were that it was to remain in my safe-keeping and handed over to you only on the eve of your wedding. She was very precise about that—that you must not have it any sooner.'

Liana looked at Felipe now. 'You know about the letter?' Her tone was censorious. It was none of his business.

'I know nothing of its contents. I know only of its existence and that it may not be opened until the eve of your marriage...' He paused and regarded her across the coffee-table. 'No doubt you will not have long to wait?'

That also, Liana decided, was none of his business. She threw him a cool look. 'You need not concern yourself. I shall manage to contain my curiosity until the appropriate moment.'

He continued to survey her, minutely, with interest, as though she were something on a slide beneath a microscope. He said, 'Your fiancé must have been rather disappointed when you gave him the news that you were staying on for a while. A girl like you...' His gaze flickered. 'He's bound to miss you.'

Liana hated it when he brought up the subject of Cliff. She could not exactly say why. It just felt like an intrusion.

She said a little stiffly, 'I miss him, too.'

'Still, his loss is my gain.'

Her eyebrows shot up. 'Your gain? In what way?'

'I am not indifferent to the company of beautiful women, and you, as you are well aware, are a beautiful woman.'

Such unashamed flattery! She was aware of no such thing! 'What I am, more accurately, is your adversary.'

'If you insist.'

'Your adversary. And your cousin.'

'As I said before, I shall enjoy getting to know you. As I said before, what's Cliff's loss is my gain.'

As he spoke, Felipe leaned towards her suddenly. Then he reached out to touch her cheek with his fingertips. And the effect was like a jolt of electricity driving through her.

As she looked back at him, all at once Liana felt stunned, as though she had been rendered rigid in her chair. A swarm of fierce emotions, strange and alien, suddenly went flooding through her.

She watched his lips move, those wide sensuous lips of his, but she could no longer hear what he was saying. All she was aware of was an almost overpowering longing to fall against the soft caress of his hand.

But then, instantly, a sense of horror tore through her. What madness had come over her? What was happening to her? She sprang to her feet, snatching Felipe's hand away.

'Leave me alone! What are you thinking of? How dare you lay a hand on me?'

Then she was turning on her heel, rushing from the room, fleeing as though from some fire-breathing monster.

And he *was* a monster, she told herself angrily as she hurried upstairs to the sanctuary of her room. Though there was something more than just Felipe that had scared her.

It was that sense of danger and excitement that he had momentarily ignited like a bush fire inside her, and that she could still feel now, however hard she sought to banish it, coiled like a hot, pulsing ball deep within her.

CHAPTER FIVE

That evening, after Felipe had gone, Liana sat out on the veranda and gathered herself together.

Danger? There's no danger, she told herself firmly as she watched the sun sink over the horizon. The worst thing that could possibly come out of all this was that Felipe would win, that she'd lose the house and all her acres and return to London empty-handed.

And she could live with that. She smiled to herself and sighed, as she leaned back in her wicker armchair and took a mouthful of her fruit juice. She had lived quite happily for twenty-four years without this troublesome inheritance, and she could carry on doing so without any problem. The things that really mattered to her would still be hers. Her home, her job, her fiancé, Cliff.

She frowned for a moment as she thought of Cliff and of Felipe's impudent claim that Cliff's loss was his gain. He didn't know what he was talking about, and, besides, the more she thought about it, the more clearly she understood the purpose of that boast.

It had been Felipe's intention by making that subtle pass at her to scare her into running back to Cliff. He thought she couldn't handle it. But he was wrong about that. Now that she'd pulled herself together, she could handle it with no trouble at all.

She hesitated at that thought, remembering how she had reacted when he had reached out and touched her cheek with his hand. That had been shock, not excitement, she decided. Simple shock at his shameless insolence.

Again she thought of Cliff, this time a little guiltily, though surely guilt was a little out of place? Nothing had happened. She'd been startled, that was all.

But she was aware, all the same, that Cliff would never understand this strange sparky relationship she had with Felipe, nor the almost perverse enjoyment she derived from it at times. And maybe that was where the guilt had sprung from. From the realisation that this was something she would never be able to share with her fiancé.

She knew what Cliff would say. He had said it to her often when her emotions got the better of her or she acted impetuously. 'It's that hot Latin blood of yours,' he would tease her kindly, always adding, 'Not that I would change you for the world!'

Liana gazed at the night sky. In the three years she had known him, she and Ciff had never once exchanged a harsh word. She had never seen Cliff angry, had never even seen him upset—and had certainly not seen him blaze with emotion, as she had seen Felipe do!

For the first time ever that suddenly struck her as a lack. Though that was ridiculous. She should be grateful he was so placid!

The night sky was full of stars. Liana frowned at them for a moment, thinking about the ranch and the problems it had brought her, and wondered what Cliff would do in her shoes. More than likely, knowing his sensible turn of mind, he would simply leave the matter in the hands of Señor Carreño. If a solution existed, let the legal experts find it. A hand-to-hand battle with Felipe Mendez wasn't going to get anybody anywhere!

So, was she being silly in her decision to stay on here? For she knew in her heart that her decision was partly rooted in the taste she was fast developing for just such a hand-to-hand battle! She wanted to beat Felipe personally and she wanted to *see* him beaten. She wanted to see him slink off with his tail between his legs.

Just for a moment that unlikely image almost made her laugh out loud. He might end up beaten, but it was not in his character to slink off with his tail between his legs! However great his defeat, he would march from the arena with that arrogant dark head of his held high and full of pride.

She smiled to herself with understanding. If it was she who was vanquished, she would do exactly the same!

A tissue-thin moon hung low in the sky. Liana frowned at it as she rose and walked to the edge of the veranda. She *was* being silly. For once she ought to act sensibly and do as Cliff would do—go home and leave the legal battle to Carreño.

At a sudden sound behind her, Liana swung round to find Rosaria standing in the open doorway.

'*Señorita, yo voy*. OK?' she asked Liana.

Liana nodded. '*Si, si*. You go home. I'll be fine. *Y gracias de todo*.' Thank you for everything, she added, pleased with her improving Spanish.

As Rosaria departed, Liana leaned against the veranda and listened to the woman's footsteps disappearing down the driveway. Tonight, Liana had insisted, she would sleep at the house alone. There was no need for Rosaria to put herself out, as she had almost demanded to be allowed to do. After all, as Liana had discovered in the course of the day, the small houses of the ranch hands were scattered all around. She could see their lights on now. She was far from isolated.

She breathed in deep the clean night air and caught an unexpected waft of Rosaria's cooking. That was one thing Liana had been unable to do—dissuade the good woman from preparing her dinner! And the results smelled absolutely delicious! So delicious that Liana suddenly felt hungry!

She straightened, drained her fruit juice and headed indoors, pausing for one last glance at the stars, aware of a sudden sense of well-being.

And in that moment, with her face turned to the sky, the balmy night air of the pampas embracing her, almost unconsciously her sense of resolve flooded back to her.

I shall stay. I shall fight Felipe Mendez. I shall enjoy every minute of it. And, what's more, I shall beat him!

Suddenly, across her head, fell a long dark shadow. From where she knelt Liana glanced up, squinting against the sun.

'I might have known!' she scowled, squashing the strange jolt that had gone through her. 'I might have known it would be you!'

'*Señorita, buenos días!*' His tone was light-hearted. 'For some reason you do not seem overjoyed to see me.'

'I'm just a very good actress, remember?' Heavy irony. 'Secretly, of course I'm overjoyed to see you!' She turned away and continued what she'd been doing, scraping out a hole with her fingers in the dusty ground. 'So to what do I owe this unexpected pleasure?'

'I want a word with you. I've been looking all over. And the last place, I confess, I expected to find you was out on the pampas, up to your elbows in dirt.'

'Is that so?' Liana smiled a pleased smile. It was positively heart-warming to discover that he'd been running around in circles looking for her!

What was less heart-warming was the fact that he'd found her. And now he was enquiring, 'So, what are you doing?'

'Isn't it obvious what I'm doing?'

What had prompted that snappy answer was the arrogant way he was standing over her, a tall commanding figure, dressed in jeans and calf-high boots, his faded cotton shirt rolled back to his elbows, his face shadowed by the wide-brimmed leather hat on his head.

When he simply smiled one of those amused, arrogant smiles of his, she elaborated crossly, 'I'm planting a tree!'

'Indeed, I can see that.' She could feel his eyes on her. 'But what I'm asking myself is why you're wasting your time performing, with a marked degree of inefficiency, a task for which I employ an army of able-bodied experts. Perhaps you would be good enough to explain?'

'Explain?' Liana lifted irritated eyebrows. 'I don't think I'm obliged to explain anything to you. You're forgetting, this is my land as much as it is yours. If I want to plant trees on it, that's exactly what I'll do—and neither you nor anyone else can stop me!'

'No one is trying to stop you, *señorita*.' The arrogant amusement in his voice was maddening. 'All I am doing is simply pointing out to you that if it is your purpose to make some kind of gesture, to inflict, as it were, your stamp of ownership on the property, you might perhaps have found a more suitable way of doing so.'

He paused a beat and from beneath the wide-brimmed hat Liana could feel the dark eyes dance mockingly over her. 'That is, is it not, what you were doing, *señorita*? Endeavouring to make some small statement of ownership?'

Arrogant pig! Liana rose to her feet, wiping her grubby hands on the sides of her trousers. She looked into his face—she could not see his eyes. 'And are you,' she put to him, her tone mimicking his own, 'endeavouring to make some small statement of ownership by coming here and making a nuisance of yourself?'

He smiled at that. He found it amusing. And Liana felt his eyes slide over her as he observed, still in that mocking tone, 'You have mud on your trousers. Digging holes and planting trees is not really an occupation for one who cares as much as you do about appearances.'

So he had not forgotten that critical exchange, conducted while she was hanging her clothes in the wardrobe! A smile touched her lips. She had been a little hard on him then. One did not go around dressed fit for tea at the Ritz when one was working on a ranch on the Argentinian pampas!

But that alteration to her thinking Liana kept to herself. To Felipe she replied archly, 'One has to make sacrifices. I decided it was worth ruining a pair of trousers for the sake of getting to know my property.'

'You call digging holes in the ground getting to know a piece of property?'

He laughed as he said it, annoying her even more. In clipped tones she informed him, 'This isn't all I've been doing. I've been on the go since six o'clock this morning...'

She gestured vaguely in the direction of the group of ranch hands who, off in the middle distance, were busily planting saplings, just as she had been doing before she was so rudely interrupted. 'I got Rosaria's husband and some of the other ranch hands to show me around and explain things to me. I've been learning quite a bit about El Dotado.'

'Rather a wasted effort, don't you think? Of what use will this scant knowledge of El Dotado be to you once you are back where you belong in London?'

Liana glowered at him. Of course she belonged in London. That was where she had always lived. It was where her work was, where Cliff was. But who was Felipe to tell her where she did or did not belong?

'I believe,' she answered tightly, 'that my knowledge will be useful. By the time I'm back in London I may well have found a way of fulfilling Great-Aunt Gloria's condition without actually, physically, being here.

'And besides, you're forgetting...' she tilted her chin at him '...my mother came from these parts. I am not a total alien. Part of me belongs here, in a way, almost as much as you do!'

'And we all know which part that is!'

The wide lips smiled scathingly. Beneath the shadow of the leather hat-brim Liana felt the black eyes glint maliciously. She looked back at him with irritation. 'And what is that supposed to mean?'

'I think you know very well what it means. The part of you that drew you to this country was not some corner of your heart searching for forgotten roots. It was a less sentimental part of you by far. It was your greedy, grasping outstretched hand!'

'Well, you would know all about that!' Liana felt her fists bunch angrily. 'As the possessor of two greedy, grasping outstretched hands, you're an expert in such matters!'

'You reckon?' With an amused smile, Felipe tilted back his hat, so that his eyes were suddenly revealed. 'And you didn't figure on bumping into an expert, did you?'

'So at least you admit it?' Liana's gaze flickered momentarily. The sudden dark force of those diamond-bright eyes of his hand had caused a strange sensation to go rushing through her. And it had not, she had to confess, been entirely negative.

His smile broadened. 'I admit to nothing, *señorita*. Surely you must know that that's the very first rule in every con man's code of practice? Deny all accusations. Admit to nothing.'

'A noble code of practice.'

'It serves its purpose. It protects those whom it was designed to protect.'

'And no doubt you learned it at a very early age.' She said it to insult him, yet realising as she said it that within the statement lay the acknowledgement of a truth she had not, till that moment, fully recognised.

Felipe was a man of great temperamental strength, a strength, one sensed sharply, that had been a part of him always. He was what he was and he knew what he was. Like an oak, he would stand firm. He would not bend with the wind.

It was the kind of strength that, normally, she would find admirable. A man like that, if he was a good man, was the kind one could depend on.

But Felipe used his strength in the mean pursuit of evil. It had to be so, that he was a con man through and through, for it would not be his way to stray into that area if such treachery were not an already established part of his character. Great-Aunt Gloria, no doubt, was only one among many who had fallen prey to his greedy ruthless ways.

The realisation both shocked her and hardened her against him. And this stiffening of her spirit was deeply reassuring.

Though, surely, it crossed her mind, she had not needed reassurance? Surely there had been no danger of her softening towards him?

He was looking down into her face with those eyes as black as ebony, scrutinising her in that infuriatingly arrogant way he had. He said, referring to her almost forgotten comment, 'I learned many things at an early age, *señorita*. Things that, in your innocence, you would scarcely believe.' His smile broadened. 'There are many things I could teach you.'

'I'm sure there are.' Liana could feel her heart beating. By his standards, almost certainly, she was an innocent—but not so innocent that she had failed to pick up the sexual innuendo in that last remark!

'But none,' she assured him, looking him in the eye, 'that I would even remotely wish you to teach me!'

And suddenly she was doubly certain of the fact that this man was a charlatan through to the marrow. What other kind of man would insist on subjecting a full-blooded, soon-to-be-married cousin to this totally inappropriate and rather tacky flirtation?

But then he surprised her. He took a step towards her. 'There is one lesson, however, that I insist on teaching...'

All sorts of strange emotions were suddenly scrambling inside her. As he caught hold of her arm, Liana's blood was racing. With outrage, she told herself, as she sought to snatch her arm away. This fierce stirring inside her was nothing but pure outrage.

As she fought to pull her arm away, she stumbled slightly and felt her body collide with Felipe's. And just for an instant, as it seemed to her he held her there, she was totally, hopelessly overcome by the physical sensations that went driving through her.

The warmth of his skin, the strength of his torso as his broad muscular frame pressed hard against her breasts. Tongues of flame licked her senses. Her breath caught in her throat. She wanted to cry out, 'Stop! What the devil are you doing?' But to her horror she found she could not speak.

Black eyes were blazing down at her, consuming her, devouring her. Liana's heart stopped inside her. A startled rabbit in a trap.

But then, to her astonishment, he was releasing his grip on her, stepping past her and, with a veiled smile, tossing down his hat. 'You need a lesson, *señorita*, in how to dig a proper hole. This one is scarcely big enough to plant a lettuce. It's no good at all for that sapling you've got there.'

As his eyes held hers for an amused mocking moment, Liana could see how much he was enjoying the way he had manipulated her. She had believed he might kiss her, and he had wanted her to believe that. Perhaps, if the ranch hands hadn't been present, he might even have gone ahead and done it. The taking of such liberties was definitely not beyond him!

But even as she stood there, almost rigid with fury at him, he had grabbed hold of the spade she had tossed aside earlier, defeated in her digging by a couple of large stones, and was proceeding with an ease that merely irritated her further to enlarge the hole to about three times its former size.

He stuck the spade into the ground and stepped back to glance at her. 'That, *señorita*, is how it ought to be done.' Then, snatching up his discarded hat, he raised two fingers to his lips and with a piercing whistle summoned one of the ranch hands.

'Now one of our paid experts will finish the job off for you,' he informed Liana, slapping his hat back on his head.

'There's no need for that. I could have planted the sapling. The hard part's done now. I could easily have done the rest.'

'I doubt that.' Felipe's eyes beneath the wide leather hat-brim regarded her with open scepticism. 'Whatever you may have talked yourself into believing, you are definitely not cut out for anything so physical as farming. Tapping away at a word processor in some air-conditioned office in the heart of London—that is what you were meant for.'

'I don't happen to live in the heart of London.' She found the picture he had drawn of her oddly offensive. 'I happen to live out in the suburbs. The room I work in is not an air-conditioned office. It's a very cosy little room that overlooks the garden.'

'The garden in which you have no doubt gained your expertise in digging holes for planting lettuces.'

'Very funny!' But Liana was laughing. He had said it with a smile, and it *had* been quite funny. And suddenly, as she looked back at him, she was struck by a strange thought.

There was really something rather remarkable about the fact that, in spite of the way they fought and bickered, the two of them were still capable of sharing a joke. They had this ability, quite spontaneously, to put hostility aside and enjoy a lighthearted moment together.

Quite involuntarily, she found her thoughts turning to Cliff. If she'd ever spoken to Cliff with even half of the sharpness that she constantly employed against Felipe, all that would now exist between them would be wounded silence. Jokes would be totally out of the question!

She found this thought a little unsettling—both the thought and the fact that she had made the comparison. Though all it demonstrated, of course, was that Felipe was thick-skinned!

Still, she turned away just a little too brusquely and informed Felipe, 'And if you'd leave me alone, I could get on with gaining some expertise in digging bigger ones!'

'Not here, you won't!' Felipe had caught her by the arm again. Only this time there was nothing even remotely sexual in the gesture.

He swung her round to face him. 'This is not a game, *señorita*, and you've already wasted enough of everyone's time. These men have better things to do than run around tidying up after you.'

He paused for an instant and with a toss of his head gestured to where, behind him, his Range Rover was parked. 'So, if you will forgive my insistence, you're coming with me now!'

Liana tried to snatch her arm away. 'Get your hands off me! Stop ordering me around! I'm going nowhere with you!'

'And what do you intend doing?' His eyes glinted beneath the hat-brim. 'Do you intend to hang around here, distracting my ranch hands, getting in their way, keeping their minds off their work?'

'They're my ranch hands, too!' That was scarcely a valid argument, but it was the way he spoke as though El Dotado were all his that really grated on Liana's nerves.

'And does that, according to you, give you the right to waste their time?'

'I wasn't wasting their time!' Liana glared back at him. 'And they weren't complaining, so why should you?'

'Of course they weren't complaining.' A slow smile touched his lips. 'I imagine it has been quite a welcome diversion for them to have a beautiful young English girl tagging along with them all day.'

His eyes drifted over her, sensuous and provocative, causing that familiar sense of discomfort to well up inside her. Then his grip around her tightened and his dark eyes hardened.

'But as their boss, I see things rather differently. I see a group of some of the highest-paid workers in the region wasting their precious time with a wilful young woman who, if she had a clue what she was doing, if she was really cut out to run El Dotado, would realise that I'm talking sense and apologise for her behaviour.'

He would never know how close he had come to persuading her.

As she listened to his argument it had slowly dawned on Liana that maybe there was something in what he was saying. She'd approached Rosaria's husband this morning in a mood of genuine curiosity, never stopping to think that her presence might be distracting. But she sensed Felipe was right. Maybe it had not been such a good idea.

And she had been about to say so, to offer a spontaneous apology...up until that moment when he had virtually demanded one! Red-hot pincers would not prise one from her lips now!

She said instead, her eyes narrowing with dislike at him, 'Let go of my arm and stop trying to bully me!'

But he had already released her before she was halfway through the sentence. In fact, he had turned away from her, as though she had never spoken, to address the ranch hand who was coming towards them.

He said something to the man in Spanish. The man responded, '*Si, señor.*' Precisely the response, Liana reflected in angry silence, that Felipe undoubtedly most enjoyed hearing—and one that he would definitely never hear from her!

'I suggest we leave now.' Felipe had turned once more to face her. The expression in his eyes did not encourage argument.

Liana did not answer. There was no point in quibbling, but she refused to give verbal acquiescence to his wishes.

She turned politely to the ranch hand. '*Gracias,*' she told him. Then, before Felipe could grab hold of her again, she walked smartly past him, heading for the Range Rover.

As he held the door open for her, she climbed in without a glance at him. And she continued to keep her eyes fixed stonily straight ahead as he switched on the engine and drove out on to the dirt road.

She would do as he wished because his wishes, she sensed, were justified. But she refused to do it with a smile on her face!

As they headed back to the ranch house, Felipe made no move to break the silence. Liana was aware of his composed dark profile, eyes never straying from the road ahead, ignoring her as though she were not even there. And, though that suited her perfectly, illogically it also annoyed her.

She turned to him suddenly. 'You said you'd been looking for me. Was there any particular reason for the search?'

He slid her a dark look, barely turning his head. 'Did you think I might have been searching for you for the pleasure of your company?'

'That never crossed my mind.' She ignored the smile in his voice. 'I thought you might, however,' she informed him acidly, 'have been searching for me for the pleasure of tormenting me.'

'I have far better things to do during working hours. That pleasure is strictly for indulging in during my free time.'

That smile again, deeply irritating.

'So, why were you searching for me? You must have had a reason.'

Felipe swivelled to look at her, as they turned into the ranch-house driveway. 'I was looking for you,' he told her, 'because I have an invitation.'

'An invitation?' Her eyebrows lifted. 'What kind of an invitation?' Surely, coming from him, it could be nothing pleasurable?

'An invitation to a dinner party to be held at my home on Friday in honour of my sister's twenty-fifth birthday.' He added quickly, lest she fondly imagine, even for one moment, that the invitation had been his idea, 'My sister is anxious to meet you. Female curiosity.'

'I see...' Liana was torn between her natural politeness, which demanded that she express her thanks for his sister's courtesy, and the oddly powerful sense of uneasiness she felt at the prospect of an evening in Felipe's company.

But before she could decide how she ought to answer, he had drawn to a halt outside the ranch house and was leaning across her to open the passenger door for her.

'A car will come to pick you up at eight o'clock,' he told her as she stepped down on to the drive. He leaned to pull the door closed and paused to smile down at her. 'If you're still here at El Dotado, make sure you're ready on time. And if you're not, if you have already flown back to London, don't worry; it will be my pleasure to confer your regrets to my sister.'

Then with an arrogant squeal of tyres he was gone.

CHAPTER SIX

A STRANGE thing happened the following morning.

Just as Liana was finishing breakfast, Rosaria appeared in the kitchen doorway to inform her that a Señor Julio Montilla was in the sitting-room, waiting to see her.

Who? Curious, Liana hurried through to the sitting-room to find a sprightly-looking seventy-year-old, with bright brown eyes in a weather-beaten face, rising from the sofa to greet her.

'Julio Montilla. At your service.'

That claim, it transpired, was quite literally true. Julio, as he proceeded to explain to Liana, in easy and perfectly fluent English, was at her disposal for the duration of her stay to show her round the ranch and tell her all about it—its history, how it was run, the financial details. Everything, in fact, that she could possibly want to know.

'I worked on this ranch for twenty-five years,' he told her, 'and for the last fifteen of these I was your aunt Gloria's manager.' The bright eyes clouded with sadness for a moment. 'Unfortunately, at the time when she began to fall ill, I was forced to retire after suffering a bad heart attack, so I was unable to help her in her hour of greatest need.'

He straightened and looked with pride into Liana's eyes. 'But we remained friends to the end and it will be an honour for me to assist you, her niece, in any way I can.'

Liana felt grateful and delighted. But there was one question she had to ask.

'Who sent you here, Señor Montilla?' She sensed she already knew the answer, though the logic behind it baffled her totally. 'Was it by any chance Señor Felipe Mendez?'

The old man smiled. 'He did not *send* me, *señorita*. He simply asked me as a favour, and it was my pleasure to oblige.'

That much was evident as they set off an hour later in Julio's battered old truck on a guided tour of El Dotado. The old man was quite obviously enjoying the whole thing every bit as much as Liana. He clearly loved every inch of the place and enjoyed sharing his knowledge, which was vast and comprehensive. There was not a question he could not answer.

He took her to the fields where crops of maize and sunflower grew and explained to her all about the sowing and the reaping, the different types of fertilisers and the machinery that was used. Liana found herself listening to him with rapt fascination.

'Tomorrow,' he told her, as he dropped her off back at the ranch house, after a busy and thoroughly stimulating day, 'I shall take you to see some of the animals we keep. We have a herd of some of the best Jersey cows in the area.'

Liana collapsed into bed exhausted that evening—too exhausted to write the letter she'd been meaning to write to Cliff!—but feeling happy and looking forward to tomorrow. Today had been a day of revelations, and one of the things she believed she had understood was at least part of the reason why Felipe had asked the old man to look after her.

With Julio in charge of her education there would be no more danger of her leading astray the ranch hands, distracting them from their work and generally wasting their time! And Julio, of course, was the perfect tutor. She had learned more about the ranch in one hour from him today than she had during the whole of the previous day.

And perhaps that was another reason, she reflected with a touch of cynicism, why Felipe had asked this obligement of the old man. Perhaps he had been hoping that such a deluge of information would convince her that she had taken on far more than she could ever cope with. Perhaps it had been his plan to intimidate her to the extent where she would throw in the towel and catch the first flight back to London.

She smiled to herself as she slipped between the bed sheets. His ploy had had quite the opposite effect. It had ignited in her an enthusiasm that had not been there previously. And she was more determined now than ever to hold on to her inheritance!

Liana leaned back against the linen pillows and with a warm glow of satisfaction reached out and switched off the bedside lamp. Felipe thought he was pretty smart, but he would never beat her.

And come Friday evening, the evening of his sister's birthday dinner, when, no doubt, he would be half expecting—and unreservedly hoping!—that, defeated, she was on her way back to London, she would look him in the eye and take great pleasure in disappointing him!

The car arrived to pick her up at eight o'clock sharp. A spotlessly shiny long white Cadillac with a driver who tipped his cap to her when Liana answered the door to him.

Liana climbed into the back seat, feeling a trifle bewildered. Felipe must have hired the Cadillac to impress her, or else it belonged to his sister or some friend. For it was beyond the bounds of imagination that this elegant, sophisticated limousine could belong to a man like Felipe Mendez, whose definition of elegance seemed to be a pair of freshly laundered jeans!

She sat back against the butter-soft leather upholstery and gazed out thoughtfully at the fleeing landscape. Over the past few days, under Julio's expert tutelage, she had come to know virtually every stick and stone of the area—at least as far as the El Dotado boundary—and she no longer felt herself to be a stranger. She had even, she reflected, developed a strong fondness for the place.

A frown touched her brow. Her sanguine mood would soon be shattered. Felipe was bound to spoil her evening.

As they rapidly crossed the boundary and passed into unknown territory, Liana shook herself inwardly and made herself a promise. She had been looking forward all week to meeting Felipe's sister, and any other relatives who might be at the dinner party. She simply would not allow Felipe to spoil her evening. He could be as rude as he liked. She would simply ignore him!

They had been travelling for almost forty minutes and Liana was starting to think that they would never get there, when at last the sleek white whispering limousine turned off the main road and through tall wrought-iron gates into a sweeping tree-lined driveway.

And then she saw it and her heart stopped inside her. A house like a palace, elegant and sprawling, illuminated by spotlights set in the grounds all around it. Compared to this, Great-Aunt Gloria's house was a shack! Surely Felipe couldn't live in a place like this?

Still blinking in surprise, she stepped out of the limousine, suddenly glad she had worn her most elegant outfit—oyster silk trousers with a matching scoop-necked camisole, pearl earrings in her ears and silver sandals on her feet. She had worried that she might be a little overdressed. She sensed now that that need be the least of her fears!

She was right. As she began to head for the main door, which was approached by a sweeping balustraded stone staircase, suddenly the door opened and a young woman appeared, dark-haired, beautiful, dressed in a stunning scarlet dress, and with a cry of delight came hurrying towards her.

'Liana! You must be Liana! I'm so happy to meet you!' She threw her arms around her and embraced her warmly. 'I'm Juanita. Felipe's sister. I'm so glad you could come!'

Liana hugged her in return, warmth flooding through her. 'It's wonderful to meet you, too,' she told her.

This is what it should feel like, she was thinking to herself, when one finally meets a long-lost cousin.

This instant sense of kinship and affection. Not the unnatural antipathy she had immediately felt for Felipe.

'So you made it, after all.'

Liana recognised his voice first. She glanced up into the doorway as Juanita led her up the steps. But as her gaze fell on the figure who stood there in the lamplight, for a moment she almost dropped dead in her tracks.

This was not the Felipe with whom she was familiar, the jeans-clad creature in casual shirt and dusty boots. Involuntarily, her jaw dropped as, wide-eyed, she gazed up at him. She could honestly say that never in her life had she seen a man look so breathtakingly handsome.

He was dressed in a sharply cut navy linen suit, with a perfect white shirt and subtly toning tie. And there was something about him that almost made her smile—the way he was standing there, black hair gleaming in the lamplight, as though he never appeared in public dressed any other way!

It was that natural black arrogance of his, she decided, pulling herself together!

'Of course I made it.' As she came level with him, she looked up at him, hating the way her heart continued to flutter. 'I wouldn't have dreamed of missing your sister's birthday dinner.'

'I should jolly well think not!' Juanita was beside her, pausing to deliver her brother a playful poke in the ribs. 'How dare you even suggest that she might have missed it?'

In that moment, as he smiled, Felipe's features suddenly softened. A look of deep and sincere affection filled his face. And there was something quite surprisingly disarming about this unexpected and spontaneous change in him. Liana had scarcely believed him capable of simple human affection. But it was clear that he dearly loved his sister.

But now Juanita was leading her across the hallway, then through an arched doorway into a splendid, glittering room. A group of guests were gathered, drinking champagne and chatting, but just as Juanita was about to introduce her, a uniformed maid appeared at her elbow and murmured something in her ear.

Juanita smiled apologetically at Liana. 'You must excuse me for a moment. A minor crisis in the kitchen.' She touched her brother's sleeve. 'Be an angel, Felipe. Introduce Liana to the other guests. I'll be back as quick as I can.'

As Juanita departed and Felipe led her towards the group, it was almost an effort for Liana to keep her face straight. The thought of Felipe passing for an angel was about as believable as a jackal sprouting wings! How well did Juanita really know her brother? Or did familial love make her totally blind?

Politely, if not angelically, Felipe introduced her. 'This is Liana,' he told them. 'A great-niece of Tia Gloria.'

A rather roundabout way, Liana thought, oddly offended, of telling them who she was without pronouncing her his cousin. He clearly still found that relationship hard to stomach.

But he was continuing in an amused tone, 'Liana lives and works in London, but she has done us the honour of coming here briefly to visit us.'

Liana slipped him a shrewd glance. He was definitely no angel! With just the tiniest of emphases on that word 'briefly' he had allowed his horns to show quite distinctly! Yet as she caught his gaze, the black eyes danced back at her, mischievously, offering to share this private joke.

And as they mingled with the other guests—at least half a dozen of whom, Liana was delighted to discover, were related to her in some way or another!—his behaviour towards her could not have been more impeccable. And more than impeccable. Generous and charming. Had she not known better, she might have believed that he was proud and pleased to have her in his home!

The other guests, too, were friendly and welcoming.

'I've always wanted to meet my cousin from England,' a moustached young man, who'd been introduced as Salvador, declared as he handed her a glass of champagne. 'And you're every bit as lovely as I imagined you'd be!'

Liana felt her cheeks pink at the compliment. 'I've always wanted to meet you, too. All of you,' she answered, realising for the first time as she said it that it was true.

The desire had not been conscious, for she had known nothing of her mother's family. She hadn't even known that all these relatives existed. But it had been there all the same, this desire she had just confessed to, buried deep inside her, just waiting to be discovered, like some secret unrecognised, unfulfilled need.

She had half expected that her remark might provoke Felipe into dropping his current highly civil façade, that in damning tones he might challenge the truth of her claim. But he surprised her as he remarked, 'Tia Gloria felt the same. She confessed to having always wanted to meet you.'

Liana turned to look at him. 'Did she tell you that?'

'She told me that often. But, alas, it was not to be.'

As his eyes held hers for just a moment, Liana searched them for the familiar signs of a rebuke. But she could see none. His gaze was oddly shuttered. All she could detect was a hint of shared regret.

How odd, she decided. What on earth's got into him? He's almost behaving as though he actually quite liked me!

But before she could reflect further on this unlikely aberration, Salvador asked her, 'How are you enjoying El Dotado? It must be very different from what you're used to.'

'Oh, very!'

Liana felt quite grateful for the diversion. That unfamiliar warmth in Felipe's eyes had thrown her.

Then someone else asked, 'Tell us about London!' And as she obliged she felt that sense of dissonance dissolve. Pretty soon, in fact, all she was aware of was how easily the conversation was flowing, and how happy and at ease she felt with her new-found relatives.

But the conversation was cut short when one of them asked, 'So, are you planning on becoming a rancher, Liana? If you are, you're off to a flying start. You couldn't wish for a better partner than Felipe.'

As she hesitated, wondering how most diplomatically to answer, two things happened simultaneously. A maid appeared, offering to replenish their champagne glasses, and suddenly a firm hand was cupping Liana's elbow and drawing her away from the group.

'Allow me to show you the gardens before we go in to dinner,' Felipe murmured, Liana guessed, more for the benefit of the others. His tight grasp on her arm really gave her little choice!

This was more like it! He was reverting to type!

Seething, but in silence, Liana allowed him to propel her across the room and through the wide french doors that led out on to a huge paved terrace. He had executed her removal with such suave subtlety that to have protested, or even to have tried to snatch her arm away, would have made her look ill-mannered and childish.

But, once out on the terrace, as soon as he had released her, she turned on him angrily. 'What the devil do you think you're doing? Were you afraid that I might expose you to your relatives as something less than an ideal partner? Were you worried that I might tell them how you're trying to get rid of me and get your hands on all of El Dotado for yourself?'

Felipe was leaning casually against the stone balustrade, champagne glass in hand, a look of innocence on his face. 'What an untrusting nature you have. *Señorita*, I simply wished to show you the gardens.'

He waved an elegant hand towards the lush lawns and bright flowerbeds that stretched down from the terrace as far as the eye could see. 'They are beautiful, are they not? As you are a lover of gardens, I felt sure you would appreciate this chance to admire them.'

He smiled as he said it. Another private joke. But Liana glowered at him. He would not manipulate her so easily. 'You forget,' she reminded him, 'I'm only interested in lettuces. And I doubt you have anything so mundane here.'

'Perhaps a few, tucked away somewhere in some corner. Perhaps you'd like to inspect them and see if they've been properly planted?'

Liana wanted to smile, but she kept her face straight. He was growing far too adroit at winning her round. She said sternly, not looking at him, laying her champagne glass on a nearby table, 'You know, this evening you almost had me fooled. You'd been behaving so civilly that I'd almost forgotten you were such a bully.'

Felipe took an unhurried mouthful of champagne. 'Did you like me in my more civil disguise?'

'I see you admit it was just a disguise.' Carefully, she refrained from giving him an answer. As a matter of fact, she had rather liked him.

More fool her! She added quickly, 'I always knew that, underneath, you're nothing but a savage.'

'Is that how you see me? As a savage?' He smiled. 'What a very romantic notion.'

'Romantic? I can assure you, there's nothing romantic about it.' She knew he was teasing her. She felt her cheeks flush. 'I have no particular liking for savages.'

There was a pause. Liana felt the dark eyes travel over her, but there was a lightness in their expression that disallowed discomfort.

Then he said, 'I suppose that's why you chose a man like Cliff. I'll bet there's nothing even remotely savage about your fiancé.'

How had he managed to make that sound like a criticism, and why had her heart flickered strangely inside her?

Liana pushed aside these questions and answered light-heartedly, 'Cliff, savage? Not even one tiny little bit. My fiancé is a gentleman to his fingertips!'

'That's what I thought. And I'll bet he treats you like a lady?'

'Infallibly.'

Felipe smiled. 'Isn't that a little boring?'

'Boring?' The suggestion had taken her by surprise.

'Yes, boring.'

'How could it possibly be boring?'

Felipe paused. His body shifted, so that he seemed to confront her. 'Wouldn't you rather be treated like a woman?'

As he held her eyes, Liana felt a strange twist inside her. She felt oddly exposed, as though he could see inside her, as though he had understood something about her she hadn't even understood herself.

She said, in an effort to cancel out that feeling, 'I don't know what you mean. You're talking nonsense. My relationship with Cliff, the way he treats me... all of it is perfectly satisfactory...'

'Is it? Isn't it just a little tedious?'

'Tedious?' She feigned surprise, but she had known he would say that. She had known he would use that very word.

She frowned at him, suddenly deeply resenting the way those dark eyes of his seemed to pierce through her head. 'Why does a relationship have to be tedious,' she challenged him, 'just because it happens to be civilised?'

'It sounds tedious to me.' He was smiling provocatively. 'It sounds like the sort of relationship I'd run a mile to avoid.'

'No doubt it is. But I'm not you. I suppose you like lots of drama in your relationships. Lots of fighting and emotion and——'

'Passion.' He held her eyes. 'Most of all I like lots of passion.'

The look in his eyes, the way they had driven into her as he had spoken that simple two-syllable word, had caused the blood in her veins to rush through her. All at once her heart had broken into a gallop and the hairs on the back of her neck stood on end.

'And what about you? Have you no taste for passion?' His lips curled at the corners. 'I find that difficult to believe.'

Liana could not hold his gaze. His eyes had stripped her naked. He could see the warmth that tingled across her skin. And more. He could see the sudden wild pounding of her heart.

She stared down at the paving stones. Almost defensively, she told him, 'I love Cliff and our life does not lack passion. Civility and passion are not mutually exclusive. It is perfectly possible to have them both together.'

'Is it, *señorita*?'

'Of course it is. Why on earth shouldn't it be?' She forced what she feared was a weak, revealing smile. What she and Cliff experienced together would not, she suspected, comply even remotely with Felipe's definition of passion. Felipe's brand of passion would be in another category entirely! The man had passion written in every virile line of his face!

Something reared up inside her, almost a kind of longing. Those lips of his, those long-fingered hands, that taut powerful body would know how to drive a woman crazy.

But, instantly, a wave of shame overtook her. How could she allow herself to fall prey to such feelings? She had a fiancé whom she loved, to whom she was totally devoted. And, besides, such feelings were perhaps a little inappropriate. Felipe Mendez, after all, was her cousin.

She swallowed hard. Perhaps she ought to remind him of the same.

Liana looked him in the eye. 'Forgive me if I change the subject, but there's something I keep wondering.' She narrowed her gaze. 'Why do you find it so hard to admit that I'm your cousin? You insist on calling me *señorita* and you introduce me to our relatives as a great-niece of Tia Gloria. Why can't you just drop the false formality, call me Liana and tell people that I'm your cousin?'

Felipe delivered her a long look. The dark eyes were suddenly shuttered. He said in a flat tone, 'Are you trying to tell me what to do? I thought we had established earlier in this conversation that I am not another civilised Cliff whose only wish is to leap eagerly to do your bidding?'

His change of mood was deeply reassuring. For a few minutes back there the atmosphere between them had become far too intimate, far too threatening. Liana met the flint in his eyes with a sense of relief.

'I'm not telling you to do anything,' she answered crisply. 'I'm simply pointing out that it's a little ridiculous to go on treating me like a stranger. After all, whether we like it or not, we are related.'

Felipe turned away as though she had not spoken. He said, keeping his back to her, 'So, *señorita*, you still haven't told me what you think of my gardens.'

That deliberate formality was almost hurtful. He really was at pains to make it very clear that he found their blood relationship distasteful in the extreme.

Liana drew her breath in sharply, surprised at how easily he had reached her. Why should she care that he disliked her so intensely? After all, her dislike of him was equally strong.

She responded without looking at him, glancing over the balustrade, 'The gardens are beautiful, even by moonlight.' She smiled and made no attempt to stop herself adding, 'I confess, I'm surprised that such beautiful gardens and this exquisite house could belong to an individual such as you.'

'A savage like me, you mean? Yes, I expect you are.' The studied insult had not touched him. 'No doubt you had assumed that I lived in a shack.'

Not a shack, exactly. But definitely somewhere much more modest. Everything she knew about him had somehow added up to that.

But she did not say that. Instead she accused him, 'No doubt it was your good fortune to inherit all of this.' Just as you had been hoping, she added silently, to inherit all of El Dotado.

He did not turn to look at her. 'As a matter of fact, I didn't. I earned all of it—the house, the garden, the land—with the honest sweat of my own brow.'

All of it? How much was there? 'You own land beyond the gardens?' In spite of herself, suddenly Liana was curious.

'A little.'

'Only a little?' Liana smiled with understanding. No wonder he was so desperate to lay his hands on her acres! As beautiful as they were, this house and the gardens would not exactly supply him with a living.

He turned then to look at her and leaned back against the balustrade. And there was something in his expression that caused her smile to fade.

In a low voice he told her, 'I own every piece of land from the boundary of El Dotado to Tierra Fe. Decide for yourself whether that is a little or not.'

Liana had no idea how many kilometres it was to Tierra Fe, though she distantly remembered seeing the name on the map. But she could recall all too well the forty-minute journey from the boundary of El Dotado to here. In terms of acreage, the amount of land to which he was laying claim, she suspected, quite easily ran into six figures!

It was as she was endeavouring to digest this staggering piece of information that Juanita suddenly stepped out on the terrace.

Apologetically, she addressed Liana. 'You must think I'm neglecting you! Please forgive me, but I see Felipe's been looking after you.' With a warm smile she took Liana by the arm. 'Let's go in now;

we're almost ready to eat. And you shall sit next to me. You're my special guest tonight.'

And so, arm in arm, the two women moved indoors, but suddenly the last thing on Liana's mind was the undoubtedly splendid dinner that awaited her. As she stepped through the french doors, she turned for a moment to look into Felipe's secretive dark face, a thousand questions racing through her mind.

If he already owned such a vast amount of territory, why was he bothering about El Dotado? Her five thousand acres were a mere drop in the ocean!

And what else had she to discover about him? she found herself wondering as he looked back at her with those unfathomable midnight-black eyes.

A great deal, she sensed. She felt a flicker of danger and turned away abruptly, struggling to stifle her curiosity. For to dig too deeply into the truth about this man would be reckless, unwise, perhaps even fatal.

Yet in spite of herself, she wanted to know. She could feel her curiosity, unstifled, unstiflable, drawing her towards him with invisible threads, though she could sense she was dancing on the edge of a precipice.

CHAPTER SEVEN

JUANITA'S birthday dinner was a great success. The food was delicious, the conversation entertaining and Liana actually managed, for at least part of the time, to drive Felipe from her mind and concentrate instead on enjoying herself.

'This is a regular event,' Juanita told her as they chatted. 'Every year Felipe lends me his house for my birthday, so I can put on a really lavish dinner. My own house is a little small. It would be bursting at the seams!'

Liana was curious about her charming new-found cousin. 'Where is your house? Is it near here?' she enquired.

'It's in a little village between here and El Dotado. I work there as a secretary for a local accountant.' She smiled. 'My father lived there from the age of seventeen, and I was born there. I love it. I wouldn't live anywhere else.'

Her brown eyes grew sad. 'Of course, my father's dead now. He and our mother died in an accident some years ago, as you probably know.' She paused for a moment, then once again her eyes brightened. 'But I have a wonderful brother. Felipe takes good care of me.'

As Liana stole a quick glance across at Felipe—surprisingly, she had no difficulty believing that—Juanita laid a friendly hand on her arm. 'You must promise to come and visit me while you're here.

Just let Felipe know when. We're in constant touch with each other.'

It was after midnight when the party started to break up.

One by one Liana bade farewell to the other guests as they made their way outside and climbed into their cars. And as she watched them go, she felt a tug at her heart. She had been showered with invitations from her relatives to visit, but would she ever see any of them again?

That depended on the outcome of her battle with Felipe. And though she was still as determined as ever to beat him, she was only now just beginning to realise how great her loss would be if she failed.

It was as the last guests were driving off that Juanita turned to her. 'You'll stay the night, of course? Please don't say no. It's far too late to drive all the way back to El Dotado. We'd both love you to stay,' she added quickly, as Liana hesitated.

As they stood facing one another in the hallway, Liana caught sight of Felipe hurrying up the outside steps towards them. She grimaced to herself. Juanita was wrong about one thing. There was probably nothing Felipe would love less than for her to stay overnight!

She smiled apologetically at Juanita. 'I was really rather planning on going straight back. If you don't mind, I think it would be better.'

'But why?' Juanita frowned at her, then turned appealingly to Felipe, as he crossed the hallway on long strides to join them. 'Liana wants to go straight back to El Dotado. Tell her she has to stay. Tell her we want her to!'

Felipe smiled a convincingly selfless smile. 'If Liana is really anxious to get back to El Dotado, I'll drive her back. It would be no trouble.'

Liana met his gaze. 'Surely there's no need for that? Couldn't your driver take me back—the one who brought me?'

'I'm afraid not. He knocked off a couple of hours ago. He's probably in bed now, fast asleep.' Felipe paused. 'The only chauffeur available, I'm afraid, is me.'

As Liana hesitated, contemplating this less than joyous option, Juanita cut in, 'Liana doesn't need a chauffeur. She's going to stay here. I absolutely insist on it.' She turned, on the verge of triumph, to Liana. 'You can borrow some of my night things. I have loads of stuff upstairs. And you can have the main guest room. I'm sure you'll be comfortable.'

What choice did she have? But still Liana hesitated. There was something about the thought of spending the night in Felipe's house that made her feel distinctly uncomfortable.

Perhaps Felipe felt the same. He smiled that elusive smile of his. 'If you insist on going back, believe me, it's no trouble for me to drive you.'

'Don't be silly. She's not going back.' Juanita was insistent. 'You're staying, aren't you, Liana?'

Liana paused another instant, then she smiled and gave in gracefully. 'OK, I'll stay,' she nodded to Juanita.

The choice, after all, was either to spend the night here or to endure a long car ride alone with Felipe. Neither solution appealed to her, but perhaps the former might be preferable.

By spending the night at his home, at least, she would not have to be around him. She would be tucked up safely in the main guest room! And tomorrow morning the driver could take her back to El Dotado.

She glanced at Felipe. 'I'd hate to inconvenience you by forcing you to drive all that way.'

He had caught the subtle irony in her tone. He smiled, just as she'd known he would, making her smile too, and responded in a tone of equally subtle irony, 'For you, *señorita*, nothing could be too much trouble.'

Juanita showed her to the guest room on the first floor—a beautiful room with a four-poster bed, all decked out in pretty rose prints. As she brought her a nightdress and matching dressing-gown, as well as a change of clothes for the morning, she told Liana, 'You'll find toothpaste and soap and stuff in the bathroom. But if there's anything you need, my room's just a couple of doors away.'

There was nothing Liana could possibly need, she soon discovered, that wasn't already on the shelves of the sumptuous adjoining bathroom. There were a couple of toothbrushes, still in their Cellophane wrappings, and jars of creams and lotions and bubble bath. It was even better stocked than her own bathroom at home in London!

She had a quick wash and changed into the pretty lawn nightdress, then glanced at the french windows that stood half open, the pale voile curtains blowing softly in the night breeze. It had been her intention to close the windows and climb straight into bed, but it struck her that she wasn't quite ready to sleep yet. In spite of the late hour, she still felt wide awake.

Lest the cool night air chill her, she reached for the lawn dressing-gown that Juanita had laid out on a nearby chair, and slipped it on before crossing to the window. Then, parting the billowing curtains, she stepped out on to the balcony—and it was just at that moment that there was a knock on the door.

'Come in!' She turned and called the invitation spontaneously. It was undoubtedly Juanita come to check that she was OK.

But it was not Juanita. Her heart jumped as the door opened and Felipe stepped silently into the room.

'I hope I'm not disturbing you?'

'No, I wasn't going to bed yet.' Automatically, she was pulling the front of her robe closed and tightly tying the belt at her waist. It was ridiculous, but all at once her heart was racing.

'I just came to check that you were comfortable.' He was still wearing his navy suit, but had loosened his tie and undone the top couple of buttons of his shirt. 'I hope you have everything you need?'

'Oh, yes, thank you. Absolutely everything.' She gestured awkwardly in the direction of the balcony behind her. 'I was just about to take a breath of air before going to bed.'

'Sounds like a nice idea.' His hands were in his trouser pockets. He smiled a disarming smile. 'Would you mind if I joined you?'

'No, of course not.'

She did, but what else could she say? He was her host, after all. She was a guest in his house. And he had totally undermined her by asking her permission. Never before had he bestowed on her such an honour!

It was a beautiful night, with a huge silver moon and a thick scattering of stars like diamonds strewn on velvet. As Felipe followed her out on to the balcony, Liana leaned against the railings, a growing turmoil inside her, and stared in confusion up at the heavens. What was confusing her was that she was strangely pleased to see him.

Then she heard him say, 'I hope you enjoyed the evening. I know Juanita was delighted that you could be here.'

'It was a lovely evening. I did enjoy it.' He was standing alongside her, but thankfully not too close. Liana breathed in deep and fought to calm her foolishness. She wasn't pleased to see him. She was simply growing used to him.

'It must have been interesting for you to meet all those undiscovered relatives. Interesting and, I suspect, a little emotional?'

Liana wanted to glance round at him, but suddenly she did not dare. That sympathetic remark, so full of insight, she realised, was the last thing she'd been hoping to hear. She would feel much easier with hostility.

She took a deep breath. 'Yes, it was,' she answered. 'It was wonderful meeting my mother's relatives. I just wish there'd been someone there who'd actually known her.'

As she spoke she felt the tension inside her ease a little. The growing warmth she had felt towards him this evening was undoubtedly caused by belated feelings of kinship. It was really nothing to feel anxious about.

She turned then to look at him. 'Your father, for example.'

'My father?'

'Your father. My uncle. My mother's brother. I would very much have liked to meet him.'

Felipe said nothing for a moment. For some reason he seemed to hesitate. Then he answered in a flat tone, 'Your uncle was a good man. One of the very best men I ever knew. He sometimes spoke about your mother. And always kindly.'

There was something odd about that answer that, in her confused state, Liana for the moment could not quite fathom. But she felt pleased to hear that her mother's brother had loved her.

She sighed. 'You know, it's a very strange thing to know nothing whatsoever about one side of one's family. Not even to know of the existence of most of them.'

He nodded. 'Yes, I can understand that.' But there was a note of odd reserve in his voice that made it impossible to tell if he really believed her.

Liana turned to look at him then and spoke with an urgency that surprised her. 'I really did have no idea that they existed. My mother never, ever spoke about her family. I knew that her parents were dead, but that was all I knew. She came to England when she was still a young girl. She was only eighteen when she met and married my father. By the time I was born, she'd been away from Argentina for twelve years. She'd become an Englishwoman. She never spoke about her past life.'

'Weren't you curious?'

'Of course I was curious. As I got older I used to ask her questions, and she would give me some kind of answer. But never any details. She never told me any stories about her life before she came to England.'

She sighed and looked into Felipe's dark-eyed face that was watching her closely as she spoke. 'I know it sounds incredible, but it's absolutely true. Perhaps it was because she was so devoted to my father. She always said her life only really began when she met him.'

Felipe smiled then, quite suddenly, as though touched by that revelation, and Liana found herself looking at him with a jolt of surprise. Surely it wasn't possible that he was a romantic at heart?

There was a pause, then Felipe spoke again, his tone oddly flat, difficult to decipher. 'And is that,' he asked her, 'how you feel about Cliff?'

She had not been expecting this sudden shift of direction. Yet her answer was firm. 'I love him, if that's what you're asking.'

'You already told me that.'

'Then there was no need to ask.'

'What I just asked was a slightly different question. Do you love him the way your mother loved your father?'

The question was insolent. It was none of his business. Yet his query touched a nerve somewhere deep inside Liana. All her life she had prayed that she might have the good fortune one day to be blessed by a marriage as happy as her parents'. And she had vowed to herself that she would never settle for less.

She tilted her chin at Felipe. 'Yes, I do,' she answered.

'I'm happy to hear it.' His eyes surveyed her boldly. 'I'm happy to hear that there is more to this relationship than the civility you mentioned earlier.'

'I already told you there was more.'

'Then I wish you joy. I hope the marriage turns out to be all you hope.'

'I wish you likewise.'

'A joyous marriage?'

'If that's what you want. And a passionate one, of course.'

As Felipe met her gaze and laughed, the momentary tension between them vanished. Then he leaned back casually against the railings. 'How are you getting on with Julio?'

It was so like him, this sudden change of direction. Liana found herself smiling as she watched him for a moment. Perhaps it was the reason, she found herself reflecting, why her conversations with Felipe at least were never boring.

She said, 'We're getting on great. He's been absolutely wonderful. He's taught me so much about El Dotado.'

'He's a fine old man. You could have no better tutor. What Julio doesn't know about El Dotado isn't worth knowing.'

'There's just one thing that puzzles me...' Liana paused and looked at him, her expression genuinely quizzical. 'What on earth prompted you to send him to me? I would have expected that was the last thing you were likely to do.'

'Which just goes to show you how little you still know me.' He smiled as he said it. 'You haven't figured me out yet.'

'Has anyone?' It was a perfectly sincere question. 'You're not the easiest man in the world to pin down.'

'Do you still find that frustrating?'

'I never said I did.'

'You're right. You denied you found it frustrating.'

'And I continue to deny it.'

But even as she said it, it struck Liana that her claim was no longer strictly true. Her continuing inability to understand him *was* beginning to frustrate her a little.

Purely out of a desire to make sense, she assured herself, of the bits and pieces of his character—some likeable, some less likeable, some endearing, some despicable—that at the moment just didn't seem to fit together.

As he watched her with amusement, she reminded him, 'You still haven't told me why you sent Julio.'

'I didn't send Julio. I simply asked him to look after you.'

Indeed. That was precisely what Julio had said. A statement, she remembered, that had had the effect of somewhat denting the image of Felipe as bully.

She rephrased her question. 'So, why did you ask him to look after me? Were you hoping to intimidate me by revealing the extent of my ignorance about ranching?'

He feigned surprise. 'Are you so easily intimidated?'

'No.'

'That's what I thought.' He held her eyes. 'You see, though you've failed with me, I've pretty well got you figured.'

Liana laughed a little uneasily. 'Congratulations. But that's not what you told me the other day.'

'Perhaps the other day I was simply being modest.' Then he added as she guffawed, 'And the only reason I spoke to Julio was as a favour to you. I was simply being civil.'

'I don't believe that either!'

'Why on earth not?'

'Because it doesn't sound like you, I'm afraid. It's far too simple and straightforward.'

'So, you see me as devious?'

Liana grew serious. 'Yes, I do. Nothing is ever quite the way you depict it.'

He let his eyes roam her face. He raised one dark eyebrow. 'So, how have I misled you, *señorita*?' he enquired.

'Well, for a start, you didn't tell me about any of this.' Liana waved an arm at the house and the stupendous gardens and the incalculable thousands of acres beyond. 'You led me to believe that you were anything but rich.'

'Did I?'

'I think you did. I think you did it deliberately. I think it amuses you to mislead people.'

'In that case you must think I have a somewhat warped sense of humour?'

Liana regarded him narrowly. No, she did not think that. In fact, she rather enjoyed his sense of humour. She corrected herself. 'Perhaps it's just me you enjoy misleading.'

'And why would that be?'

'I suppose because you don't like me.'

'And why don't I like you?'

'Because you believe I'm a gold-digger.' She frowned for a moment, as an idea struck her. 'And that's another way in which you deliberately misled me. You wanted me to believe the same about you, that you were a greedy and penniless nephew trying to cash in on Great-Aunt Gloria's death by getting your hands on El Dotado.'

'And you no longer believe that? That I was trying to cash in?'

'How could I believe that now? Now that I've seen all of this!' Liana cast her eyes again around the land that stretched before them. 'Compared to all of this, El Dotado is a flea bite. You'd have to be pretty petty to want it so badly, to go to all the trouble of trying to elbow me out of it, just for the sake of what it's worth.'

And, at least, there was nothing petty about him. She thought it, though she did not say it. The sins of which Felipe was guilty would not be petty ones. They would be of the jumbo-sized variety!

The black eyes were watching her, deep and glinting in the moonlight. 'So, if not out of greed, why do I want El Dotado? Why am I trying to elbow you out, as you so delicately put it?'

'I don't know.' She thought about it for a moment. 'Maybe it's just out of spite against me. As I said, because you think I'm a gold-digger.'

Felipe shifted slightly. He let his eyes drift over her. Silence for a moment hung softly between them. Then he smiled. 'But I no longer think that, *señorita*. I would indeed be misleading you if I did not make that quite clear.'

As he said it, he had reached out one hand towards her and touched her cheek lightly with his fingertips.

'I believe your claim that you knew nothing about your family. I believe that Tia Gloria told you nothing in her letters about El Dotado or the fact that she was dying.' His fingers cupped her chin, their touch strong and gentle, yet igniting her skin as though they were a firebrand. 'I have no idea why she chose not to tell you, but she was a wily old lady and she could be secretive at times.'

'You mean that? That you believe me?' Her sense of relief astonished her. Until that moment Liana had believed she didn't give a damn about what Felipe thought of her.

Felipe was nodding. 'Yes, I mean it.' His fingers lightly stroked her chin. 'So, set your mind at rest. I don't believe you're a gold-digger.'

Liana was aware that her heart was beating strangely, yet that she was behaving as though there was nothing strange happening. As though there was nothing the least bit reprehensible about the fact that they were standing here in the moonlight, eyes locked together, Felipe caressing her face, and she suddenly possessed of a fierce dark yearning that all at once had reared up like a caged beast inside her.

His eyes poured into hers. He was smiling softly. Then he bent towards her suddenly. 'I think it's time to say goodnight.'

The dark eyes, so close, were like cinders, scorching her. The fingers around her jaw all at once had tightened. And as the blood roared inside her, Liana could not move. With a small helpless sound she closed her eyes.

His kiss was so fleeting that it was as though she had dreamed it. Yet that momentary pressure of his lips against hers was like an explosion of her senses. She longed to press herself against him. She longed to demand more.

'Goodnight, Liana.'

He was drawing away now. She had to lean against the balcony railing to support herself.

'Goodnight,' she managed to say through the confusion that possessed her. She felt shattered, her emotions shredded and tattered, strewn like torn paper all about her.

How could she have felt that longing that had possessed her? It was wrong. It was shameful. Only Cliff should stir such feelings. And certainly not Felipe; Felipe, who was her——

She did not finish the thought. As he stepped through the french windows and turned for an instant to look into her face, another, even more shattering thought took its place.

Suddenly she knew.

Suddenly all of it made sense.

Liana wanted to call him back, but all her strength had deserted her. She leaned against the railings, her heart frozen within her. To know the truth, she had always sensed, would be a dangerous thing. And now that she knew it she was afraid to her very soul.

Liana slept somehow, though she woke a dozen times, peering endlessly at her watch, longing for morning. The revelation that had come to her on the balcony last night was accurate, she was certain, but she had to confirm it.

She rose ridiculously early—just after seven—showered quickly and changed into the jeans and T-shirt that Juanita had left out for her last night.

Then she hurried downstairs, grabbed the first person she saw—a young maidservant who was polishing the marble-tiled hallway—and demanded, 'Where is Felipe? *Donde esta Señor Mendez?*'

'*Afuera.*' Out. It was the answer she had half expected. But never mind, she would not move from this house until she saw him.

Two hours passed. She drank coffee and picked at some breakfast. Her insides were churning. It was impossible to think of eating.

Then Juanita appeared, still in her dressing-gown. 'You're up early. I thought you'd still be asleep.' Then she paused and frowned at Liana's expression. 'What's the matter? Has something happened?' she enquired.

Liana gathered herself together. She must handle this more coolly. She smiled. 'Not at all. There's just something I want to ask you.'

Five minutes later, she had her confirmation. She did her best to take it calmly, hiding the storm inside her, as Juanita poured more coffee and remarked calmly, 'I thought you knew.'

And now what? As Juanita went off to get dressed, Liana debated with herself whether to go or stay. The driver was at her disposal whenever she wanted, waiting to take her back to El Dotado, and there was no need for her to see Felipe. Juanita had told her all she needed to know.

She rose from the breakfast table and began to hurry from the room. She would go upstairs to say goodbye to Juanita, gather up her things and then quickly be gone. For it was better that she did not come face to face with Felipe. Not now. Perhaps not ever again.

But as she stepped into the hallway she almost collided with the tall dark figure who was heading towards the breakfast-room. He caught her by the arms, as though to stop her from stumbling, and looked down at her with amusement in his face.

'Where were you off to in such a hurry?'

'Home!' She bit the word at him, her eyes like lances. She tried to shake free of him. 'Far away from you!'

He had not let her go. 'Any particular reason?'

'A very particular reason. You're a liar and a cheat, but I have finally discovered the truth about you!'

'What truth is that?'

'That you're not my cousin! That you're not related to me even remotely! Go on, deny it, if you dare!'

The black eyes looked down at her. His hands still held her firmly.

'No, I am not your cousin and we are in no way related.' He pulled her almost roughly towards him. 'So, what do you suggest we do about it?'

CHAPTER EIGHT

FELIPE had grabbed hold of Liana as though she were a rag doll. As though he might pick her up and toss her over his shoulder and carry her off to some murky, unknown fate—though why *that* particular scenario was the one that instantly occurred to her, Liana was too confused at that moment to figure out.

Dark eyes flashing, Felipe repeated his question, 'Go on, tell me, *señorita*, now that you know we are not cousins, what do you reckon we ought to do about it?'

'Do about it? Do about it?' Liana glared at him, struggling to free her arms from his grip. 'I don't reckon we ought to do anything about it! I'm just angry that you didn't tell me the truth in the first place!'

'Why, what difference would it have made?' Fiery-eyed, he surveyed her. 'Would our relationship have progressed any differently if you had known that your mother's brother was not my father?'

'No, of course not! All I'm saying is that I think it most peculiar that you didn't make the truth plain from the start!'

'Peculiar? And that is why you are so angry and upset? Simply because you find my behaviour peculiar?'

'Yes.' She had to force herself to continue to look at him.

His eyes flickered with dark amusement. '*Señorita*, I do not believe you.'

'And what other reason could I have?'

'That is for you to know, not me. I cannot see inside your head.'

'There's nothing to see.' Her heart was beating strangely. Angrily, she tried to tug her arms free. 'Now kindly let go of me. Immediately!'

Felipe shrugged and released her, as though he had intended to anyway. 'There! Now you are free.' He smiled an amused smile. 'Free to do whatever you choose.'

His gaze lingered as he said it. The wide mouth curled with devilment. There seemed to be a hidden invitation in the statement.

Liana felt the discomfort within her increase. She took a step away from him. 'What I choose to do is leave here! And, since that is precisely what I was about to do anyway before you so inconveniently waylaid me, if you don't mind, I shall now proceed!'

He smiled at her pomposity. She had almost smiled herself. 'I wouldn't dream of stopping you. So, proceed,' he urged her. He stood aside and watched as she strode quickly past him, heading across the hall towards the staircase on her way up to her room to collect her things.

'There's just one problem...'

'What kind of problem?' Liana paused on the first step and turned to look at him.

'Well, more of an inconvenience than a problem, really. Nothing that can't be sorted out...'

He was teasing her, toying with her, enjoying keeping her in suspense. Liana breathed deeply to control herself. 'What exactly are you talking about?'

Felipe had stepped towards the staircase and was now leaning against the banisters, smiling a deliberately infuriating smile. 'I'm talking about how you intend to proceed to leave here.'

'By car, of course. With your driver.' If he said 'proceed' once more, she vowed, she would hit him!

'Ah. That's the problem...'

Liana glared and said nothing. She would not play this irritating little game of his.

'You see,' he continued, as she waited, 'my driver isn't free to take you back to El Dotado. Unfortunately, I've just sent him on another errand.'

'Deliberately, I expect! In order to inconvenience me! You knew I was relying on him to take me back!'

He ignored her reprimand. 'However, as I say, there's an easy remedy. Once I have finished one or two small chores here, I shall take you back myself.'

'I see! I'm now stranded here to wait at your convenience!' Fury lashed inside her. She had been planning to escape him, and now, instead, he had made her his prisoner. 'I suppose you're feeling very pleased with yourself?'

He shook his head. 'No more than usual.' The more irritated she became, the more he enjoyed it. 'Are you in a hurry? Do you have some appointment?'

Liana scowled across the banister at him. 'That is neither here nor there. I don't need a reason to go home when I want.'

She had said it without thinking. And not for the first time. The word 'home' had tripped from her lips quite naturally. And just for an instant she forgot about Felipe and all the annoyance he was causing her and reflected that it was true—El Dotado had become like home.

'I won't be long. I just have to make a few phone calls.' Felipe had stepped away and was glancing at his watch. 'I'll be ready to leave in about forty-five minutes.'

Then he was turning away and striding back across the hall.

In fact, it was slightly less than forty-five minutes. Just over half an hour later, as Liana and Juanita were chatting together over a cool drink out on the terrace, Felipe appeared and told her, 'Ready when you are.'

'Don't forget you promised to visit me before you leave,' Juanita reminded her as they embraced and said farewell. 'I'll never forgive you if you don't.'

'Oh, I won't forget, don't worry,' Liana reassured her, as she climbed up inside the big Range Rover. 'There's no way I plan to leave without coming to visit you first.'

As she slammed closed the door she stole a glance at Felipe, who was revving the engine and slipping it into gear. She could just guess at the question that was going through his head: How soon exactly are you planning to leave?

He did not voice it, however. In fact, he did not speak at all as they swept off down the driveway and headed for El Dotado. Perhaps he was planning, it occurred to Liana, to pass the entire journey in silence. Perhaps he was not in the mood for discussions.

Well, that was unfortunate. She slid her gaze round to glance at him. She had not the slightest intention of remaining silent. On the contrary, she intended remaining anything but silent. She had questions to ask, and she would demand answers.

Liana sat back in her seat, her mind buzzing and humming. She would make him pay. He would not get off scot-free. She would question him and needle him and drive him crazy. She would disturb his equilibrium as hers had been disturbed.

She stared out at the rushing landscape for a moment—the fields, the trees, the rich red earth. Then she said, 'Last night, when you said I didn't know you, I didn't realise to what extent you were speaking the truth.'

'Didn't you?' His eyes didn't even flicker in her direction.

'But then, how could I?' Liana glared at the dark profile. 'How could I possibly have guessed at all the things you were concealing?'

She had known he was a mass of seething contradictions. A wonderful brother, according to his sister. A thoughtful employer, according to Julio. Funny, likeable, humorous, charming. Yet this same man for years had allowed Great-Aunt Gloria to struggle with the running of El Dotado by herself. This same man had misled Liana about the nature of their relationship.

What it all added up to was nothing but confusion—but a confusion Liana was now determined to get to the bottom of.

She took a deep breath. 'You know,' she told him, 'I always used to think that you called me *señorita* simply out of your pathological dislike of me.' Liana turned to look at him as she said it. 'I thought it was simply a way of imposing a distance between us.'

He met her eyes. 'Well, it was the wrong explanation.'

Liana glanced away. 'Yes, I know that now.'

'It was perfectly proper of me to adopt that small formality in view of the fact that you are not my cousin.'

'So, why didn't you tell me?' Liana flung him a harsh glance. 'Why did you bother to keep it a secret?'

'I didn't keep it a secret. I simply omitted to tell you.' The black eyes swivelled round to her. 'There was no need for you to know.'

'I think there was!'

'Why, what did it matter?'

'It didn't matter, exactly. I didn't say it mattered!' She felt a charge of discomfort at the question, and at the answer she could feel forcing itself on her mind. Crushing it, she accused him, 'I just think it rather odd that you omitted to tell me something so fundamental. Even Juanita was surprised. She thought I knew the story.'

It was a simple enough story. Felipe's mother had married Liana's uncle after the death of her first husband, Felipe's father. Felipe had been all of eight years old when he had become Liana's uncle's stepson.

Almost to herself, Liana observed, 'And the coincidence of surnames didn't help me to guess the truth. It was sheer chance that both of your mother's husbands happened to be called Mendez.'

'A happy chance,' Felipe observed. 'Juanita and I never had the inconvenience of being known by different surnames. Not that it would have mattered,' he added swiftly. 'In my heart I have always thought of her as my full sister.'

'It's a pity you didn't feel the same closeness for Great-Aunt Gloria, particularly since she obviously thought of you as her real nephew!'

'I did feel close to her. I did think of her as my aunt.'

'Is that why you neglected her? Is that why you left her to struggle on her own for years?'

'I did not leave her to struggle on her own for years.'

'Oh, yes, you did! You're forgetting you admitted to me that you never went near her until just a couple of years ago!'

'I am not forgetting.' He turned then to look at her and the eyes that met Liana's were dark with emotion. 'I did not go near her before because I did not know her.'

'How could that be? I don't believe you!'

'I did not even know of her existence.'

His eyes burned into her. He was telling the truth. In spite of herself, Liana was suddenly quite sure of that.

Again she said, but quietly, 'How could that be?'

Felipe drew a deep breath and turned his eyes away from her. 'The reason was very simple. A family feud,' he told her. 'Some disagreement between your uncle and Tia Gloria's husband. I never got to the bottom of what actually happened, but the two sides of the family were at war for many years. I grew up, as did Juanita, not even aware that Tia Gloria and her husband existed. I only found out by accident, after your uncle was dead. I have always regretted that I did not learn earlier. I grew to love the old lady a great deal.'

For a moment Liana was silenced, taking in what he had just told her. In a small voice she said, 'And that was when you began to help her?'

'I wish I could have helped earlier. By the time I came on the scene she'd been struggling on her own for many years.' In a gesture that gave vent to all the regret and frustration that Liana could sense was burning inside him, he banged the steering-wheel with the heel of his hand. 'Perhaps if I could have taken over the running of the ranch a little earlier she might have survived a few more years.'

'You did all you could.' Liana knew that instinctively. And suddenly her earlier theory about him, already severely dented after seeing his own property last night, was lying in hopeless tatters at her feet.

She had already questioned her initial assumption that he was after El Dotado for what it was worth. Whatever reason he had, it must be some other. But she had not, until this moment, discarded her judgement that he was nothing but a heartless, uncaring nephew, who had left an old lady to struggle on her own. Nothing, she now realised, could be further from the truth.

But it was partly his fault that she had believed that false theory. She said, almost resentfully, 'You let me believe you neglected her. Why didn't you explain to me that that wasn't the case?'

'I had nothing to explain. Not to you, not to anyone.' Almost roughly, he changed gear as they turned a sudden sharp corner. 'It was up to you to believe whatever you wanted to believe.'

That made her feel small, just as she deserved. She had condemned him as guilty on no evidence at all.

'I'm sorry. I'm really sorry.' The apology came from her heart. That she had judged him so unfairly made her feel deeply ashamed.

But Felipe was not interested in her apologies. Almost harshly now, he turned to look at her. 'Don't worry about it,' he told her in a crushing tone. 'What you care to believe of me is of no importance whatsoever.'

No, of course it wasn't. She had always known that. Yet the cruel, uncaring way he had said it had felt like a spike being driven through her heart.

A foolish reaction, Liana chided herself as they lapsed into silence for the rest of the journey. She ought to be well used to his antipathy by now.

It was a relief when the ranch house at last came into view. Liana was reaching for her things, one hand poised on the door-handle before they were even halfway up the drive.

'Thanks for the lift.' As they drew to a halt, she pushed the car door open, getting ready to jump down. 'I hope it didn't inconvenience you too much.'

Liana had expected that he would just turn around and drive straight off again. It was certainly what she had been hoping he would do. But, to her dismay, he was switching off the engine. Without looking at her, he said, 'I'd like to come inside for a moment.'

Liana felt her heart sink. 'I thought you'd be in a hurry to get back?'

By way of an answer he had pushed his door open, stepped down on to the driveway and slammed the door shut. On arrogant strides, he was heading for the front door.

'First I'd like a beer,' he said.

Liana followed after him, her heart a tangle of emotions. Hurt, regret, anger, sorrow. She wanted to be alone. Why did he have to torment her?

By the time she caught up with him he was in the drawing-room, helping himself to a can of beer from the fridge-bar.

He ripped off the tab, tossed it in an ashtray and raised the can of beer to his lips. 'I hope you don't mind my helping myself?'

'Not at all. You can help yourself to a glass, too, if you like.'

'No, thanks. I prefer it straight from the can.'

Of course he did! Because he thought it annoyed her!

Liana tossed her bag on to a nearby chair. She was beyond being annoyed. She felt emotionally drained.

She was aware, though she did not look at him, that he had turned to face the window. And then, finally, he said it.

'So, when are you leaving?'

Liana almost burst out laughing. This was the question she had been expecting when they had climbed into the car after saying farewell to Juanita. Had he really been bottling it up inside him all this time? No wonder he was in such a filthy temper!

With a mocking smile directed at his back, she sank disdainfully on to one of the armchairs. 'When I decide,' she answered cryptically. 'And I haven't decided yet.'

'Well, I think you should start deciding. I think you should start deciding soon. You're wasting your time here. Go back to London.'

'I shall...' She paused and let the seconds tick by until he had half turned round to look at her. 'I shall... as soon as I decide it's time.'

He laid down his beer can. '*Señorita*, it is time now.'

She could not see his eyes. They were hidden in shadow. He was standing with his back to the light. But she could sense the implacable driving black power of them. Something turned over with a shiver inside her.

'Don't try to tell me what to do.' All at once her mouth was as dry as sawdust and her heart had begun to pound against her ribs. Yet her voice was clear and strong as she added, 'I shall stay here until I have good reason to leave.'

'You have good reason now.' He took a small step towards her. Then he stood very still. 'I would advise you not to linger.'

Quite unconsciously, Liana's fingers were gripping the chair arms. She could feel the blood hammering in her veins. She said—and suddenly her voice was not so steady, 'Neither on this, nor on any other issue, do I need your advice.'

'Perhaps you are right...' Still he had not moved.

Liana stared with hot eyes into his face. 'I can assure you I am. That is something you can take my word on.'

The broad shoulders seemed to shrug. She could feel his eyes drive through her. 'Perhaps, then, it is something other than advice that you need...'

Liana's fists clenched. Without moving he seemed to have stepped closer. Suddenly she was wishing she was standing up to face him.

But she felt glued to the chair cushions as he continued, 'Perhaps what you need is a little persuasion.'

Persuasion? Persuasion? The word swam in her head. And suddenly, as he moved, she could once more see his eyes. They caught hers and held them with a power that was almost physical.

For a moment time seemed to lie suspended all around them. There was no movement, no sound, not even the ticking of a clock. It seemed to Liana that for that moment even the natural rhythm of her breathing had stopped.

Then the dark eyes that had ensnared her seemed to grow darker. Liana knew what was about to happen. Her heart spurted inside her. Then, as he reached out one hand and plucked her from the armchair, she fell against him with an unresisting sob.

His arms were about her, drawing her closer. And the power of him was beautiful, too beautiful to resist. Her arms circled his neck, her heart weeping with the wanting of him. Then all at once every inch of her was bursting into flames as he bent and crushed his lips against her lips.

A storm drove through her, a storm so momentous that it tore the breath from her lungs and the strength from her body. She *had* to hold on to him or she might have slipped from the planet. Her will, her strength of being had all melted away.

And yet, and yet... There was a strength blossoming inside her that she had never experienced before. As Felipe's mouth clung to hers, fierce, compelling, this strange new power was reaching up inside her and spreading through her until it possessed her totally.

It was the power of life, the power of being, the power that drove her very spirit. And all at once it was pouring through her like a torrent, filling her heart to overflowing.

Something in her had awakened, something both spiritual and deeply sensuous. She could not resist it. She did not want to. She longed to surrender herself to it, body and soul.

Felipe's hand was on her breast, increasing her sweet torment, causing the blood to surge through her veins. And as his fingers plucked and teased the hardened nipple and she felt her body press hungrily against him, a cry of bright longing escaped from her lips.

'Oh, Felipe! Felipe!'

Her fingers tore at his hair. What he was doing to her was so delicious that she could not bear it to stop.

The touch of his lips was so hot it burned her. She could feel his warm breath like fire against her skin. And as his lips grazed her cheekbones, her chin, her throat, every inch of her seemed to be melting with pleasure—and with a desire so fierce that she could not control it.

And then, just as it seemed that this wild dream would swallow her, with a violence that froze her, he was grabbing her by the wrists and holding her out at arm's length to scowl down into her face.

'Now do you understand why you must leave here?' His black eyes lashed her, harsh and merciless. 'Now do you understand why you must go?'

For one long endless moment he continued to hold her, then, almost roughly, he released her.

'You are another man's woman and it is not in my nature to take what I know belongs to another! But if you continue to tempt me, I shall do so, *señorita*! So, leave! Go back to London. And go back immediately!'

Then, even as she stood there, stricken and breathless, he had turned on his heel and was striding from the room.

CHAPTER NINE

BY LUNCHTIME, when Julio came to pick her up, Liana had pulled herself together. And she had made sense in her mind of what had happened earlier.

Felipe had caught her off guard. That was all there was to it. He was a desirable man and she had responded instinctively. But, in the end, all they had done was exchange a few passionate kisses—which ought not to have happened, but was scarcely a calamity. There had been no danger of his taking what was not his. Cliff was still the man she loved. The man she would be faithful to, always.

Yet Felipe had now forced her to face something she had been avoiding—the power of the physical attraction between them. She had sensed it, but never had the courage to admit it. And all those lies he had allowed her to go on believing had helped to keep the truth at bay.

The myth about their kinship, his supposed neglect of Great-Aunt Gloria that had filled her with such dislike and contempt for him. These had been the bricks of the barrier that had kept her safe.

Some bricks! Some barrier! How easily it had crumbled! Yet how fiercely she had clung to it!

Too fiercely, she now forced herself to realise. For one thing, their supposed kinship had really been no barrier. Intimacy, even marriage, between first cousins was not exactly the most uncommon occurrence in the world! Yet she had used the belief that they were related to deny the fact that she found Felipe attractive. And that was what bothered her more than anything.

For surely her love for Cliff ought to have been shield enough to protect her from the temptations of Felipe? Why should it have mattered to her one way or the other whether Felipe was her blood relative or not?

As she rode with Julio now through the ripening maize fields, Liana wrestled uncomfortably with that thought. Though perhaps she was being unnecessarily hard on herself. After all, she was fallible flesh and blood. She was here on her own, thousands of miles from her fiancé, and Felipe was a powerfully attractive man. She would have to have been made of stone not to be aware of it!

Inwardly she sighed and tried to concentrate a little harder on what Julio was telling her about fertilisers and topsoil. What this agony over Felipe actually boiled down to was the fact that she must never be caught off guard again!

For she had no intention of obeying his command to get on the first plane back to London. Now she knew the dangers, she would simply learn to deal with them. They would not scare her away as Felipe had obviously been hoping.

But from now on she must be careful. Very careful. If this was his new tactic to frighten her off—one, in fact, that he had used before, but less violently, with less vigour—then she would have to be doubly careful to keep him at a distance.

She was suddenly aware that Julio was asking her a question. With an effort, she pulled herself back to the present. 'I'm sorry,' she told the old man, 'I didn't catch that.'

He smiled and repeated what he'd been suggesting—that they stop off at the nearby *confiteria* that served the ranch workforce during the day and have themselves a refreshing cup of coffee.

Liana forced a carefree smile. '*Si, vamos*. Let's go.'

But inside she was struggling to squash a nagging fear. Keeping Felipe at a distance was not going to be easy!

Two days passed without her seeing Felipe, two days during which Liana began to relax a little. Then a letter with hopeful news arrived from her lawyer. There just might be a way for her to hang on to her inheritance.

'Come to my office on Thursday morning,' Carreño told her at the end of his letter, 'and I'll explain to you more fully what the solution might entail.'

Liana drove to Trenque Lauquén on Thursday morning, full of a burning, impatient excitement and intensely aware of the change that had come over her.

Once, her only reason for fighting for El Dotado had been in order to thwart Felipe. That was no longer the case. She had grown to love the place. To say goodbye to all of it now would be a terrible wrench.

She left Carreño's office on a cloud of bright optimism. The solution he had proposed would not be easy to implement, but with determination she was certain she could do it!

She had lunch at El Matador, the *confiteria* where she had stopped off for lunch on her previous visit—only to have Felipe barge in on her so rudely!—and this time enjoyed her wine and steak uninterrupted.

Then she went to the ENTEL office, hoping to share her news with Cliff, only to be told by his secretary that he'd be out of the office all day. So she left a message. 'Tell him I called and that I'll call again. And be sure to give him my love.'

After that she went for a walk around the town—though it was siesta time and most of the shops were closed. But it was fun just peering into the shop windows, acquainting herself with the layout of the town, admiring the sun-scorched buildings with their pretty verandas.

She was in a relaxed frame of mind as she went to pick up the Shogun and headed back along the dusty road to El Dotado. Her problems were all about to be solved soon, she sensed.

How wrong could you be? Her problems hadn't even begun yet! And she knew that the minute she turned into the driveway of the ranch house!

The Range Rover was parked arrogantly outside the front door, as though it had every right to be there. And Liana just knew, even before she had marched round the veranda, that she would find its owner sitting outside the sitting-room with a can of beer from her fridge-bar in his hand.

She was absolutely right, except that the beer was in a glass. He was evidently not bothering to assume his rough and ready image today!

Felipe smiled when he caught sight of her, that teasing, seductive smile of his that made her defences fall away. 'At last,' he said. 'I thought you were never coming.'

'Have you been here long?'

It was spoken as a reprimand, though her tone, she was aware, had been unnecessarily harsh. But it was the only way she had felt able to hide the breathtaking sensation that had swept through her like a hurricane the instant she had looked into his face.

It was a feeling she could put no name to, but just for a moment it had made her soul weep.

Liana thrust the feeling from her and added, glancing at his beer glass, 'I see, however, that you've made yourself at home.'

'I knew you wouldn't mind. I know how hospitable you are.' His eyes travelled over her, making her skin jump. 'And to answer your first question, I've been here about an hour.'

Liana turned away. She felt oddly hot and bothered. Learning to handle herself and her responses to Felipe was not going to be quite as easy as she'd hoped.

'I'm thirsty. I need a drink.' She stepped through the french windows, glad to put some distance between them, as she headed for the fridge-bar in the sitting-room.

He called after her, 'There's plenty of beer. I brought a crate with me, just in case your resources were depleted. I wouldn't like you to accuse me of being some sort of free-loader.'

Liana pointedly ignored him and poured herself an orange juice. A crate! she was thinking. I just hope it's not his intention to hang around here long enough to drink it!

That surge of negativity had a salutory effect. As she returned to the veranda, Liana was gratefully aware that her foolish palpitations had subsided.

She seated herself in one of the cane chairs opposite him. 'So, to what do I owe this unexpected little visit?'

He smiled into her face, taking a mouthful of his beer. 'Do I have to have a reason? Couldn't my motivation simply be that I couldn't bear to be away from you for a single moment longer?'

That was in very poor taste. Liana delivered him a hard look.

But Felipe could be a master of poor taste when he wanted to be. He added, as she glared at him in disapproving silence, 'Perhaps I couldn't wait to pick up where we left off.'

'I seem to remember we left off with you walking out the door. I think that was a perfectly satisfactory ending.'

He smiled as though he had detected the confused blush she had sought to smother. 'An ending?' He held her eyes. 'You didn't just see it as an interlude?'

'Definitely not.' Liana's tone was brittle. The fingers around her glass had gone stiff. She glared into his face. '*Why* did you come here? I hope for your sake it was not for the purpose you've just suggested.'

'You hope for my sake... That sounds like a warning.'

'That's more or less what it was intended to be. I won't tolerate any more of that kind of behaviour!'

'Tolerate?' Felipe smiled and leaned back in his chair, regarding her with evident enjoyment. Lazily, he stretched his long jeans-clad legs out in front of him, raised his glass to his lips and watched her over the top of it.

'Tolerate, you say?' He repeated the word, savouring it as one might savour a stumbled-upon jewel. Then a coarse look touched his eyes. '"Oh, Felipe...! Felipe...!" The way you moaned my name the other day did not sound a great deal like toleration to me.'

Liana felt the heat of shame rush up on her. How could he be so base as to remind her of that? She stared into her orange juice, wishing she could drown in it, resisting the urge to throw it in his face.

She said in a cold voice, 'Why have you come here? To amuse yourself by trying to humiliate me? Or to demand once again my immediate departure?'

He said nothing for a moment, though she could feel his eyes on her. When he spoke, his voice was oddly matter-of-fact. 'No,' he told her. 'I have come to you with a solution.'

'A solution?' She glanced up then. 'What on earth do you mean?'

'I mean that, after a great deal of consideration, I have arrived at a solution to your dilemma. A solution that will allow you to retain what you have gained here *and* your life and your future in England.'

Liana opened her mouth, on the verge of telling him that she had already sorted out her dilemma by herself. But she stopped herself in time. First, she decided, let's hear a bit of what he has to say.

She took a mouthful of her orange juice. 'In that case, you'd better tell me.'

Before answering, Felipe crossed his booted feet at the ankles. His dark eyes narrowed as he looked across at her. Then he astonished her by telling her, 'I intend to buy you out.'

'Buy me out?'

'Buy you out. For a very generous price.'

Liana felt totally baffled. 'But why would you do that? You seemed, just a very short time ago, to be absolutely certain that you could lay your hands on my share without parting with a single centavo.'

'I have since changed my mind. I have decided that would not be fair. Tia Gloria evidently wished for you to benefit from her will—I'm sure she did not envisage the legal entanglements involved—and so I think it is only right that we come to some financial agreement.'

He had it all worked out. But he had misjudged her. 'But I don't want to sell,' she told him.

'Come, come.' Felipe smiled a knowing smile. 'Don't be so hasty. We have not yet discussed figures.'

'But I don't need to discuss figures. I don't want to sell.'

Still he did not believe her. He named an astonishing figure. 'I can have the money ready for you in a couple of days' time.'

Liana blinked across at him with a sense of growing suspicion. He really must want El Dotado very badly if he was prepared to offer such an enormous sum. Perhaps, she wondered, it was worth more than she had realised? Perhaps there was an oil-well underneath!

All the more reason for her to hang on to it! Not that it had ever crossed her mind to do anything else!

So she assured him, 'I'm afraid you're wasting your time. As I keep telling you, I have no intention of selling.'

He regarded her intently. 'I can go a little higher.' He named another figure, even more impossible. 'But don't get greedy, that's my absolute limit.'

Liana delivered him a steely look. 'Greed doesn't come into it. It's just that selling, quite simply, does not come into my plans.'

'And what are your plans?' His expression had grown shadowed. He was not pleased that she had turned him down so flatly.

'My plans are to stay on here.' She paused a moment. Then, deciding that she might as well go ahead and tell him what she and Carreño had discussed that morning, she advised him, 'My lawyer tells me he may have found a way.'

'For you to stay on here? You mean you plan to move in here permanently?' The expression in his eyes was little short of horror.

That was oddly wounding. Liana glanced away a moment. Then she straightened her shoulders and met the dark gaze again. 'No, I do not intend to move in here permanently. My real home and my future, as you already know, are in London. But what I intend to do is arrange my time so that I can spend a few days every month here fulfilling my obligation to contribute to the running of the place.'

She laid down her orange juice with a sense of satisfaction on the cane table. 'Señor Carreño tells me that might very well be an acceptable solution.'

Felipe's reaction was not at all what Liana had been expecting. He burst out laughing, throwing his head back. 'You mean you intend to spend your time flying backwards and forwards across the Atlantic just so you can keep your hands on El Dotado?'

'That is precisely what I intend.'

'Then you must be crazy. You'll be eating up all your profits from the ranch on air fares!'

'I'm aware that my expenses will not be inconsiderable. But I've thought about it and I believe that the sacrifice will be worth it.'

His expression had changed again. 'What are you up to?' The straight black eyebrows drew together. 'What you're saying makes no sense. Especially in the light of the offer I've just made you.'

'It makes sense to me. My considerations are not financial. As long as I break even, I don't really care.'

He had leaned forward in his chair. He had even laid down his beer glass. Every atom of his attention seemed to be focused on her. 'You've lost me. If your considerations are not financial, what the hell are they?' he demanded.

'My reasons are sentimental. Purely sentimental. I want to keep my ties with this place intact.'

She had expected him to laugh again. But he did not. Not immediately. Instead, a cynical smile began to curl around his lips.

'You mean to tell me,' he put to her, 'that in the space of a couple of weeks you have become so emotionally attached to this place that you are prepared to disrupt your life in London in order to spend a few days a month here?'

Then he did laugh, dismissively, as though the very idea were absurd. '*Señorita*, you are out of your mind!' he told her.

There was something rather enjoyable about his reaction. For once, she had succeeded in throwing him utterly. He had never in a million years expected this!

Liana took a mouthful of her orange juice. 'You may think so. You have every right to think me crazy. But that, nevertheless, is what I plan to do.'

'I know someone else who'll think you're crazy. Cliff, your fiancé. He's going to love this!'

But Liana had already considered Cliff's reaction. She told Felipe, 'Cliff will understand that it's important to me, and he'll respect that. He won't object.'

In response, Felipe let out a gasp of impatience. All at once he had catapulted to his feet. 'Well, he damned well ought to! And he ought to do more than just object! He ought to take you in hand and give you a good talking to!'

'You mean tell me what to do—the way you're always trying to do?'

'I mean talk some sense into your stupid stubborn head and give you a lesson in what having a relationship means. Don't you give a damn about what your crazy selfish plan will end up doing to the two of you?'

He was standing over her, wrath leaping from every pore of him, as though he might grab her from her seat and shake her till she rattled. And why, Liana wondered, was he taking it all so personally? What did it matter to him about herself and Cliff?

As coolly as she could—for his fury was truly daunting—she answered what she believed. 'My plan won't harm us. Fortunately, Cliff and I don't have the sort of possessive relationship that no doubt appeals to your sort of temperament. We don't feel it necessary to put handcuffs on each other.'

'I'm not talking about handcuffs! I'm talking about sharing! I'm talking about two people living their lives as one!' His eyes sparked down at her. 'Without even a word to him, you've just turned down a financial offer that could make a substantial difference to your life together. You don't even think it's worth asking his opinion!'

Liana glared at Felipe. 'I don't need to ask his opinion! I happen to know Cliff very well! If I'd thought he would disagree with my decision, I would not have turned you down so instantly.'

'Are you sure of that?'

'Of course I'm sure!'

Her decision was not the one that Cliff himself would have made, but, as he had told her so often, when it came to El Dotado he was prepared to accept whatever decisions she made.

Felipe held her eyes a moment. Then he breathed in deeply. 'OK,' he acknowledged. 'I'm prepared to believe you.' Then he narrowed his black eyes at her. 'But, all the same, you are mistaken if you seriously believe you can make this plan of yours succeed.'

'And why am I mistaken?' Inside, suddenly, she was trembling. His anger had felt like a physical assault.

'Because you cannot run El Dotado on a few days every month. I would have thought that was something you would have learned by now. Farming, ranching, is a full-time occupation. You have to be there when you're needed, not when you find it convenient!'

'I would make myself available twenty-four hours a day, so I could always be contacted if there were decisions to be made!' This was something else she had thought about, for of course she was aware that farming was not a nine-to-five job.

She glared at him. 'We're not living in the Dark Ages, you know! There are such things as telephones and faxes these days! Even when I was in London, I would always be reachable!'

'Reachable, hah!' He dismissed her argument without even taking a moment to consider it. His black gaze raked her. He stood over her for a moment, looking down at her with a face like thunder.

Then he leaned towards her. 'What are you up to?' he accused. 'It seems to me that you are playing games, *señorita*. Is this some kind of little ego trip you're on?'

And what was that supposed to mean? Liana clenched her fists and forced herself to look back at him unblinkingly.

'I have no idea what you're getting at. Kindly explain yourself,' she demanded.

'With pleasure.' The wide lips curled maliciously. 'I think what's at the bottom of this is that you fancy yourself in the role of *patrona* of a ranch in exotic Argentina. Something to impress your London friends with. I reckon that's what this is really all about. As I said. An ego trip. All the rest, all that other stuff about being so anxious to maintain sentimental ties here, all of that is just worthless garbage!'

'And how would you know that?' His impertinence was staggering! 'I suppose you can see inside my head? How can you possibly know what I feel for this place?'

'I don't have to see inside your head. I know that two and two make four. If you really cared about El Dotado, you would agree to my proposal, you would sell me your share. You wouldn't be putting forward some half-baked arrangement that doesn't have a snowball in hell's chance of working and can only do El Dotado damage in the long run!'

'You don't know that! You're simply assuming it because you feel duty bound to oppose everything I say!'

'This time you're wrong!' He tossed his dark head at her. 'The only thing I feel duty bound to do is to make sure that El Dotado continues to be run profitably, providing a living for the men and women who work on it. That's the only thing I've ever cared about! And it is for that reason alone that I will not allow this ridiculous, hare-brained scheme of yours to go ahead!

'So, be warned!' He stood over her like a towering Colossus. 'Follow Carreño's advice, spend thousands of pounds jetting backwards and forwards across the Atlantic for six months... But at the end of that six months I shall contest your right to ownership, and, you can take my word for it, I will win and you will lose. You'll be left with nothing, not one single stick or stone, not even one tiny grain of the dust of El Dotado!'

Liana's heart had stopped inside her as, with that thunderous prediction, he turned on his heel and on violent strides headed for the stairs that led down from the veranda. A kind of numbness had settled inside her.

At the top of the stairs, he swung round once more and paused to deliver one final salvo. 'By the way, my offer to buy you out is now withdrawn. You can forget about that. I wouldn't pay you one centavo! On the contrary, I intend to see you leave this place empty-handed!'

Liana did not move as he strode off down the stairs. Her brain was torn in two. She wanted to feel angry. She wanted to stand up, raise her fists in defiance and yell after him, 'You'll never win, you bully!'

But she was immobilised by the vision of implacable black anger that she had seen raging from his face. That he disliked her she had never doubted, and in a way she had grown to accept it, even though he had made it plain that he was sexually drawn to her. But what he had just demonstrated went far deeper than mere dislike.

He hated her. With a vengeance. With every fibre of his being. He hated her with a violence that was passionate and terrible.

She heard his car door slam as though it might bounce off its hinges, then the squeal of angry tyres as he headed down the driveway. And suddenly, through her numbness, she could feel herself sinking into an endless dark well of misery and despair.

It made no sense, but she could not fight it. With a stifled sob, Liana leaned back in her chair, closed her eyes and let the tears pour down her cheeks as a rushing storm of helpless grief blew through her.

CHAPTER TEN

THREE days had passed and no sign of Felipe. He had done another of his disappearing acts.

All the better, Liana decided. She did not want to see him. She could not have borne the sight of that angry, hate-filled face.

But what to do now? Was there any point in staying on? She had learned all she could about El Dotado from Julio—at least, all she could learn on a short-term stay. There were still volumes she didn't know, she was well aware of that, but they would have to be learned through practical experience, through day-to-day involvement in the running of the ranch.

That thought made her return again and again to all the things that Felipe had said to her.

Her plan to involve herself in the running of the ranch on a long-distance, strictly part-time basis he had described as hare-brained, half-baked and ridiculous. Was it? she wondered. Or was he just being obstructive because he wanted her out of the scene?

She would hate to think that, as he had suggested, the result of such an arrangement might be to damage El Dotado. In that respect her interests were identical to his.

And then there was the long-term situation to think of. Even if the arrangement proved to be practicable, in six months' time where would she stand? Would she, as Felipe had so direly threatened, have spent thousands of pounds travelling to and fro across the Atlantic only to end up empty-handed?

Carreño, after all, had offered no guarantees that the plan he had suggested would satisfy the law courts if it came to a contest between Felipe and herself. The best he had been able to offer her was that it *might*.

That left her with what appeared to be the most sensible option. Forget the whole thing. Go back to England as though none of this upheaval had ever happened and avoid what amounted to the very real risk of throwing away a sum of money she could definitely ill afford.

It was glaringly obvious. It was the sensible thing to do. But she could not quite gather her courage to do it. The thought of packing up and leaving this place forever throbbed inside her like a bruise.

And it was this mood of indecision that held her like a vice that had stopped her making another trip to Trenque Lauquén to call Cliff back as she had promised. Quite simply, she didn't know any more what to tell him. She was going round in circles, chasing her own tail.

On a wave of frustration, after breakfast that morning she climbed into the big white Shogun and just drove. All she wanted was to escape from the sense of oppression that weighed down on her, crushing her ability to think rationally, as she endlessly paced the wooden veranda.

Everywhere she looked, she seemed to see Felipe's face scowling out at her, full of malice. Why did he hate her? she asked over and over. Why had he set himself so implacably against her?

And why did she care so very deeply that he did? Why did she suddenly seem to have lost the will to fight him?

She drove around the fields where sunflowers bloomed, then across to the other side to where the cattle roamed. Less than three weeks ago this place had seemed so alien to her, as alien as the dark side of the moon. And now it was as familiar as the back of her hand.

She smiled. All her life she had believed she was a city girl—a city girl with a love of gardens. Who would ever have thought she could feel so at home on the pampas?

Just before noon she stopped off at the *confiteria* for a cup of coffee, a beef *empanada* and a chat with the ranch hands with whom, through Julio, she had made friends.

But that didn't help her mood. It only made her feel more wretched. She got back into the Shogun and drove some more.

It was the early afternoon heat that drove her back to the house eventually. In the car it was quite cool with the air-conditioning turned up full, but when she had climbed out to stretch her legs for a bit the sun had been so strong that she had been forced to dive straight back inside again! The thought of a long cool drink out on the veranda suddenly had enormous appeal.

But as she drove through the front gates, she almost turned tail again. For parked in its usual arrogant fashion, directly outside the front door of the house, was Felipe's all-too-familiar Range Rover.

What was he doing here? As she parked her own car next to it, a swarm of disorganised emotions swam through her. A sense of anxiety. She could not bear more anger. A sense of excitement that was totally illogical. And an even more illogical sudden spurt of hope.

Perhaps he had come here to apologise to her, to retract the cruel things he had said. In a warm flush of silly optimism she suddenly realised just how much such an apology would mean to her.

Liana pushed open the car door, her chest tight with emotion, yet with the flicker of a foolishly happy smile on her lips. But as she stepped down on to the driveway that flickering smile died as the figure of a man suddenly appeared on the veranda.

It was not who she had been expecting.

It was not Felipe.

It was Cliff.

'How did you get here?' Liana stood stock-still and stared at him. 'Why didn't you let me know you were coming?'

Cliff was standing at the top of the wooden veranda steps, dressed in light trousers and a smart white shirt, his short fair hair glistening in the sunlight.

He pulled a face and smiled down at her. 'What's the matter? Aren't you pleased to see me?'

'Of course I am!' What was she thinking of? Liana rushed forward, taking the steps two at a time, threw herself into his arms and kissed him. 'You surprised me, that's all. I thought I was seeing things!' She hugged him hard. 'It's wonderful to see you!'

It was at that moment that Felipe stepped out through the front door.

He barely glanced at Liana. Instead, he addressed himself to Cliff. 'I'll leave you now.' He extended his hand in farewell. 'It was nice meeting you. I hope we'll have the chance to meet again.'

'I hope so, too. And thanks for everything.' Cliff smiled at the taller man with the sun-darkened skin. A smile, Liana sensed, of genuine warmth.

And that surprised her a little. Though she had never actually thought about it, she had expected that Felipe would be as rude and overbearing with her fiancé as he habitually was with her. But that was evidently not the case. It was only her he hated. Foolishly, she felt that thought scuff at her heart.

A few minutes later, after Felipe had driven away—still without ever once glancing directly at Liana—Cliff told her the story of how he had arrived.

'I faxed Carreño from London before I got on the plane and he in turn got a message to Felipe. When I arrived at Buenos Aires there was a message waiting for me that Felipe would pick me up at Trenque Lauquén. I gather the buses from there are somewhat infrequent! And we arrived here about a couple of hours ago.'

They were out on the veranda, seated on the cane chairs, each of them sipping a glass of cool beer.

Liana squinted across at Cliff. 'You make me feel so guilty. You've gone to all this trouble because of me—because I didn't call you back as I said I would.'

Cliff smiled. 'I confess I was a little worried. I hadn't heard from you—not even a letter—for over a week. And then, when I missed that phone call and you didn't call back, I decided it was time I got on a plane.'

As Liana frowned apologetically, he leaned towards her. 'I know there's no phone here and the post is irregular. I'm not blaming you. And I understand you've been very busy...'

He took her hand. 'It was an impulse, really. I suddenly realised I was missing you and wanted to see you.'

As she listened to him, Liana had felt a growing sense of awkwardness. She wanted to answer, 'I missed you, too.' But she could not quite bring herself to speak such a lie. For the cruel, shocking truth was that she hadn't really. She had thought about him certainly, though not as often as she ought to have done, and definitely with no great sense of longing.

She said, forcing a smile, 'I've been so busy you wouldn't believe it! I could never have realised there was so much to learn about a ranch!'

Cliff leaned back in his chair and smiled across at her with those gentle understanding blue-grey eyes of his. 'Tell me about it. I'm interested,' he urged her.

Gratefully, Liana launched into an account of the days she had spent with Julio learning about El Dotado, about her visits to Trenque Lauquén, about the new kind of life she had been learning about.

Yet all the time she was intensely aware that this light-hearted chat was simply a device for delaying the moment when she would finally have to force herself to face up to something far more important. There were some serious questions she would have to start answering.

Why, for example, had she reacted as she had when she had seen Cliff step out on to the veranda? Why hadn't her heart soared with joy at the sight of him? Why, instead, had something seemed to go numb inside her?

And it was not as though, even now, the feeling had passed. As soon as she had hugged him she had felt it diminish. There had been an honest warm surge of affection for him and a genuine feeling of pleasure at seeing him.

But that was all. There had been no sense of excitement. It had felt like greeting an old friend, not the man she was to marry.

As they chatted, she tried to push these feelings from her. Surely this strange lack of emotion she was experiencing was due simply to the fact that she had not seen him for some time, that she had been absorbed in a totally new way of life, far removed from the usual life they shared, and that he had caught her off guard, turning up the way he had.

That must be it. She clung to that explanation. All the other feelings she'd used to feel for him would soon return.

They spent the rest of the afternoon quietly at the ranch house—Cliff, understandably, was tired after his long journey—then they had dinner, cooked by Rosaria, out on the veranda.

'How long do you intend staying?' Cliff asked her as they drank coffee. Oddly, so far, the subject had not arisen, though he had told her he had to be back in a couple of days.

Liana sighed and smiled at him. 'Maybe I'll go back with you. I was thinking I probably ought to go back soon, anyway. There's not a great deal of point now in staying on here.'

'I think you're probably right.' Cliff's tone was sympathetic. 'From what you've told me about the situation—that business about the condition attached to your inheritance—I think you've probably done all you can do from here. We'll just have to see if we can work out some way of making it possible for you to commute between two continents.'

'Wouldn't you mind that?'

'Not if it's what you want.'

Liana sighed. 'It is, but I think it's impossible. He'll only challenge me in six months for my share of El Dotado. And, knowing him, he'll almost certainly win.'

'You mean Felipe?'

Liana nodded. 'He'll do anything to stop me. And all that'll happen is that I'll lose thousands of pounds.'

Cliff leaned across the table and laid a hand on her arm. 'I'll help you out financially if that's what you're worried about. If it means so much to you, and I can see that it does, I reckon it's at least worth giving it a try. So, don't worry about the expense of it. Just you do what you want.'

Liana looked into his face, tears rising in her throat. There was no way in the world she would ever allow him to gamble his money on such a risky venture. But she felt deeply grateful and unworthy of his generosity.

'Thank you,' she told him. 'You're far too good to me.'

And as she looked into his eyes, she told herself firmly that that feeling that was missing would come back soon. It *has* to, she promised herself with a kind of desperation.

They spent the following day driving around the ranch, with Liana proudly demonstrating her knowledge to Cliff.

'We get two crops a year,' she told him, pointing to the maize fields. 'Wheat and oats in December, and sunflower and maize in March. And the soil is so fertile we scarcely have to use any fertiliser. The topsoil is several metres deep.'

'A little different from Muswell Hill.' Cliff caught her eye as he said it. 'I hope you're not going to find it too hard settling back to suburban life again?'

Liana laughed and shook her head, though the same thought had occurred to her. 'Don't be silly,' she protested. 'That's where I've always lived!'

'But you love this place, don't you? I can see it in your face.'

'Yes, I do.' As she said it, she suddenly remembered Felipe's accusation that the role of *patrona* of a ranch in Argentina was simply one that she fancied out of vanity, something with which to impress her London friends.

How little he understood her. And how well Cliff, by contrast, did. She leaned towards her fiancé on an impulse and quickly kissed him.

'I'll fly back with you on Sunday,' she said. 'I've made up my mind.'

* * *

The invitation was delivered by hand next morning. 'It's from the Señorita Juanita,' Rosaria told her as she handed it to her. 'Señor Felipe asked me to bring it to you.'

Liana knew before she opened the envelope what it contained. And she knew also that she had no choice but to accept. After all, she had promised Juanita faithfully that she would pay her a visit before she left.

The invitation was to dinner that very same evening, the last evening before she and Cliff were due to fly back to London.

'How splendid!' was Cliff's response when she told him. 'I'm looking forward to meeting this cousin of yours.'

Liana tried to squash the sudden nerves that were afflicting her. She, too was looking forward to seeing Juanita. But what she was dreading was the thought that Felipe might be there.

Why? she asked herself sternly as she got ready that evening, in a simple slim white dress that flattered her suntan. What does it matter if he's there? Why should I care? I shall simply ignore him. And with Cliff at my side he's hardly likely to make trouble!

Yet her anxiety persisted as they set out for Juanita's. More than anything she longed for the evening to be over.

Juanita's little house was the prettiest in the village—whitewashed, with green shutters, and tubs of flowers at the front door. And most pleasing of all, as far as Liana was concerned, there was no Range Rover parked outside, nor even a white Cadillac, no sign of Felipe at all.

She felt her spirits lift a little. Perhaps, after all, fate would be kind, and she would be permitted to enjoy her last evening in peace.

Their hostess, as Liana had expected, had gone to a great deal of trouble. Inside the house the most delicious aromas could be detected wafting from the kitchen. A bowl of *sangria* had been prepared as an aperitif, and Liana accepted a glass gratefully. She loved the traditional punch-like concoction.

And as she sipped it, she noticed that the table in the adjoining dining-room with its crisp white cloth and table-centre of fresh flowers was set for three people and not four. Inwardly, she put up a heartfelt prayer of thanks.

They chatted for a while and drank their *sangria*, then Juanita led them through to the dining-room. And it was just as Liana and Cliff were taking their seats that suddenly the front doorbell rang.

Liana held her breath as Juanita went to answer it. Surely not? Not when she was just starting to enjoy herself? Surely fate could not be so cruel?

But a moment later she heard his voice—offering what sounded like an apology in Spanish—and Liana felt a plummet of despair inside her. The hands in her lap all at once were clenched tight.

And then, as she sat there, sick to her soul, he came walking in through the dining-room door, a tall dark figure in a light blue suit, his hair black and glossy, a light smile on his lips.

The violence of Liana's reaction shocked her. As she looked into his face, the blood leapt within her and her heart felt as though it might fly from her breast.

And that was when she knew.

A sense of horror filled her. Stricken, she stared down blankly at her plate.

'What a nice surprise!' Juanita had come into the room behind him. 'Felipe thought he wasn't going to be able to make it, but here he is, after all! It's just as well I made enough food for four!'

'Knowing you, you probably made enough for a regiment!' Felipe cast an affectionate eye towards his sister. He smiled at Cliff. 'I'm sorry I'm late.'

'Don't worry, we hadn't started yet.' To Liana's deep dismay, Juanita was laying a place for him between her own place and Liana's. As he took a chair from against the wall and seated himself next to her, suddenly she was finding it difficult to breathe.

I shall have to leave. I shall have to find some excuse. The words were swimming round in her head. There was no way she could sit there next to him all evening and behave in a sane and sensible fashion.

'I decided I couldn't possibly miss your farewell dinner.'

As he spoke, Liana could feel the warmth of him, as though he were pressing up against her. She shifted slightly and half turned to look at him, but the remark, she instantly realised, had been addressed to Cliff.

So, he planned to ignore her. That would make things easier. Perhaps she would survive the evening, after all.

In the event, he did not exactly ignore her, but neither did he, even once, address her directly. And on the few occasions on which he actually looked her in the eye, his expression was shuttered, carefully detached. It was as though she were an ornament or some piece of furniture, some inanimate object of no importance whatsoever.

In a way, it made it easier for Liana to survive the evening, but at the same time his indifference rubbed her heart raw.

For she knew now. She knew beyond any doubt. And it was a truth she would have given her life not to know. It was as though something inside her were bleeding away.

As they finished coffee and Juanita started clearing up, Liana jumped to her feet, eager to be gone from the table. 'Let me help you,' she offered. But before Juanita could reply, Felipe had intervened.

'If you don't mind, Liana and I need to have a little talk. Business.' He glanced at Cliff. 'I hope you don't mind? This will be our last opportunity before you leave.'

'Of course. Of course.' Cliff nodded in agreement. Then he smiled at Juanita. 'I'll help you clear up.'

Liana stood stiffly by her chair as Juanita and Cliff proceeded to carry plates and things into the kitchen. Her heart was thundering. What did he want of her? All she wanted was to escape.

Unhurriedly, Felipe rose from his chair. 'Let's go outside to the garden,' he suggested. 'I could do with a breath of fresh air.'

Typically, he did not bother to wait for her response. Before she could answer, he was unhurriedly crossing the room to the open french windows that led outside.

Reluctantly, Liana followed. Whether inside or outside, she did not wish to speak with him alone. But inside, within earshot and sight of Cliff and Juanita, she might just have felt a little less vulnerable. Perhaps, she wondered suspiciously, that was why he was taking her outside.

She stood in the open doorway, her heart in a fierce turmoil, and watched him cross the little patio, with its scattered tubs of bright geraniums, and seat himself in one of the white garden chairs. And he seemed to be mocking her as he glanced up at her and assured her, 'Don't worry, you're quite safe. I don't intend to eat you.'

That made her feel foolish and annoyed at herself. Was her discomfort really that plain to see? She stepped forward on brisk steps. 'That thought had not occurred to me. I was just wondering what on earth you could possibly have to say to me.'

'I told you. Business.'

'Actually, you told Cliff.' She hesitated for an instant by the side of the chair opposite him, wondering what had prompted her to make that distinction. It had sounded quite embarrassingly peevish. As though she cared that he had been virtually ignoring her all evening.

'It was intended for your ears also.' He had picked up her touchiness. She could see that in his eyes as they pierced through her. But what surprised her was the lack of arrogant amusement. She had expected an accompanying disparaging smile.

There was not the faintest trace of a smile, however, as he added, 'Surely you could not think that my reason for wishing to speak to you could be anything other than strictly business? To my knowledge we have nothing personal to discuss.'

Liana had seated herself. 'Nor to mine,' she confirmed quickly. She was trying to feel relaxed, but she felt stiff and awkward. 'But I thought that, business-wise, we'd said all there was to say.'

'Did you?' He stretched his long legs out in front of him. His elbows were on the chair arms, fingers loosely laced together. He was as relaxed, she thought in misery, as she was stiff and tight. 'Well, alas,' he added, eyeing her, 'that is an opinion I do not share.'

'Why, what do you want to talk about?' She could not stop her poor heart's drumming. Every time she looked at him she wanted to weep.

'About El Dotado. What else?' he responded, still in that cool tone that cut her heart to pieces. 'I am entitled to know your plans regarding the ranch.'

He would know soon enough. She let her eyes drift away from his. This evening she had come to an irrevocable decision regarding her inheritance and El Dotado. But she could not tell him yet. First she must speak to Cliff. Cliff, as her fiancé, had the right to be the first to hear the decisions—all of them—that she had made.

She glanced up at Felipe. 'I have to talk to Cliff.'

'Haven't you had plenty of time to do that?'

Yes, but during that time she hadn't been aware of what had been revealed to her this evening. Her heart swelled inside her. She repeated, 'I have to talk to Cliff.'

'When?' He was impatient. 'How long am I to be expected to wait for you to come to some decision? A week? A month? Someone has to run the ranch——'

'I know that.' In a firm tone, Liana cut in. 'I'll wire you my decision as soon as I get back to London.'

He smiled then. 'So, you have already made up your mind. This supposed consultation with your fiancé is nothing but a subterfuge, a ploy to keep me in suspense.'

'Believe what you like.' The allegation annoyed her. In his vanity he really did believe that every move she made was somehow influenced by him.

Something broke inside her. Her annoyance was misplaced. That belief of his was alarmingly close to the truth.

She found herself saying, as though to placate him, in an effort to bring this conversation to a close, 'As I said, you will have my decision immediately—and I have reason to believe that you will not be displeased by it.'

Black eyebrows lifted. 'Do I take that to mean that you are planning to relinquish that preposterous plan of yours to run El Dotado from a drawing-room in London—with, of course, the occasional flying visit to Argentina?'

Liana hardened her gaze against him. That word 'relinquish' had struck a sensitive chord within her. Did he but know it, there was much she planned to relinquish. And her plan to run the ranch part-time from London was among the least important items on that list.

She breathed deeply and slowly and responded in a firm tone, 'Don't try to push me into discussing things now. You'll have my decision as soon as I've spoken to Cliff.'

He did not try to push her. He leaned back in his white chair. 'Poor Cliff,' he said. 'I wouldn't be in his shoes for anything. He's going to have a miserable life married to you.'

'Don't worry about Cliff.' Liana felt numb as she said it. She wanted to leap up from her seat and flee from him. But she knew that her limbs would have buckled beneath her. She clenched her fists at her sides. 'Cliff will be just fine.'

'You mean *you'll* be just fine. You don't care about Cliff. You don't love him. The only person you love is yourself.'

He spoke the words harshly. They tore at her heart. She could feel it bleeding like some poor wounded creature within her. Part of what he had said was beyond denial. That shameful part about her not loving Cliff. That realisation, to her inexpressible sorrow, had crept up on her gradually over the past few days, though only tonight had she finally, honestly, faced it. She cared for him as a friend, but without depth, without passion.

But the other part of Felipe's accusation, the part about her only loving herself, ironically, could not have been further from the truth.

At this moment she loathed herself—and for two good reasons. For her lack of love for Cliff, a man who deserved her love, and for the staggering truth that had come to her this evening when Felipe had walked into the dining-room and she had looked into his face.

In that moment she had felt a surge of love so painful that it had felt like a physical thrust to the heart.

I love him, she had known then. Deeply. Passionately. With a love so total that it consumes every part of me.

She looked with pain now into those dark contemptuous eyes of his. She loved him as she had loved no man before in her life.

Somehow, she rose to her feet, though her legs felt like sawdust. She looked down at him, her heart pulsing with misery inside her. 'I think that concludes our little chat. I think we've said all that needs to be said.'

'Have we?' Her heart ballooned with panic inside her as he rose to his feet to stand beside her. He reached out and caught her arm. 'Are you quite certain?'

For a moment the endless black gaze consumed her. The hand on her arm burned into her flesh. And just for an instant she longed to fall against him and reveal the cruel torment in her breast. Tears swam behind her eyes. I love you, she longed to confess.

But she was saved as Cliff suddenly appeared in the doorway.

'I think it's time we were on our way,' she heard him saying. 'We have an early start tomorrow morning.' He paused just an instant. 'That is if you've finished discussing business?'

'We've finished.' Even as Liana was pulling herself together, Felipe had released her and was stepping away. His expression was cool, composed, unreadable. 'We were just about to come in,' he added.

The next fifteen minutes or so, to Liana, were a blur.

She went through the motions of thanking Juanita for her hospitality. And she smiled convincingly when their hostess expressed the hope that it would not be too long before they met again.

Then she was climbing into the Shogun with Cliff at the wheel and heading back to El Dotado, knowing that her life had altered forever.

As soon as they were back in London, she would do what was right, what was only fair to both Cliff and herself. She would break off their engagement. It would be kinder, she had decided, to wait till Cliff was back on his own home ground.

Then she would wire Felipe and inform him of her decision to withdraw entirely from El Dotado. Not only did she not intend to pursue her plan, she was prepared to sign over her share to him immediately.

For there was no way in the world she could be part of an arrangement that would of necessity bring her into contact with Felipe. That would only, inevitably, bring about her own destruction.

Her mind was firm on that. For as long as she lived she must never again set foot in Argentina. And, above all, she must never see Felipe again.

CHAPTER ELEVEN

LIANA had done all the things she had promised herself she would do. And now, six weeks later, she was about to embark on a new life.

A new life. A new career. Alone, and heartsore.

The most painful part had been breaking off her engagement, in spite of the fact that Cliff had surprised her.

'You're right,' he had told her. 'Though I hate to admit it, a marriage between the two of us just wouldn't work. That vital spark is missing for you. I've always suspected it, though I hoped I might be wrong, that it was in there somewhere, that you just weren't showing it.'

Liana had felt helpless with remorse. 'I'm so sorry, Cliff. I never intended to deceive you. I used to think that what I felt for you was enough.'

'But then you discovered that it wasn't.' He had smiled a wry smile. 'You discovered that when you were suddenly afflicted by the real thing.'

'The real thing?' Liana had glanced away guiltily. She had not mentioned her love for Felipe to Cliff. There was no need for him to know about that. She had been afraid that it would only hurt him more.

But he had surprised her further. 'I knew,' he had told her. 'I knew you'd finally discovered the real thing the very first time I saw you with Felipe. It was shining in your eyes as plain as a beacon.

Every time you were with him, or even spoke about him, I could see it lighting up your face.'

'But how could you?' Liana had been taken aback. 'All I ever did was fight with the wretched man!'

Cliff had shaken his head. 'It was there all the same.' Then he'd sighed. 'Right now, I'm feeling more sorry for myself, but I'm also sorry it didn't work out for the two of you. I liked the guy, even though I knew he'd stolen your heart.'

Liana had thought long and often over the past few weeks of those kind, perceptive words of Cliff's. So, he'd known, even before she'd known herself, that she had fallen in love with Felipe!

Though perhaps that wasn't true. Perhaps she had known all along.

Hadn't she always been aware of how alive he made her feel? As though he had awakened something vital within her. And hadn't there always been a shadow of uneasiness inside her whenever she and Felipe were together, as though, unconsciously, she had been aware of what was happening to her and was terrified of what it meant?

And no wonder she'd been terrified! To fall in love with a man who disliked and despised her, as Felipe did, was surely the ultimate in masochistic folly! She ought to have fled before her heart was totally lost.

Such wisdom, however, had come a little late. Her heart *was* lost, totally and forever. And that was something she was just going to have to learn to live with.

How she was going to learn to live with it she could not begin to contemplate. The pain inside her was too huge, too raw. To allow her thoughts to dwell, even for a moment, on the engulfing love she felt for Felipe was to be seized by an agony that tore her heart to pieces.

Mercifully, there had been no further contact between them. As promised, within days of her arrival back in London Liana had sent Felipe a wire, renouncing her share of El Dotado. There was no way she could fulfil the condition of inheritance, so it was pointless dragging the whole thing out.

There had been no direct response from Felipe, just a letter from his lawyer saying that the telegram had been received and its contents duly noted.

More than likely that would be the end of it, Liana decided, for she had written also to Carreño, informing him of her decisions and giving him permission to sign any necessary papers on her behalf. Just like that, her links with Argentina had been severed.

But not her links with the South American continent. Too large a part of her now belonged there for her to turn her back on it completely. And that was why she'd made the decision she'd made.

For a year, she had decided, she would put aside her career as a freelance journalist in London and spend her time travelling around Latin America, gathering material for a book.

Her first stop was to be Brazil, and that was where she was headed now—on her way to the airport to catch her flight to Rio.

It had been a big decision, but an easy one to make. For one thing, it was a challenge, and right now a challenge was what she needed. Something to keep her mind off the pain in her heart.

She had spent the last five weeks on a super-intensive crash course, learning Spanish and Portuguese, and she felt confident now that she could get by in both these languages. And she had let out her flat to help finance her project. The new tenants had moved in literally as she was moving out!

As the taxi cab sped her towards Heathrow Airport she felt a spurt of quiet optimism through the pain that had become a part of her. Perhaps something good would come of this new beginning—though perhaps to call it a 'beginning' was a little inaccurate, since she was still a long way from leaving the past behind. There was a part of that past—Felipe—that would always be with her.

Liana cast that thought from her, fighting the emotions that swarmed within her. She must not think like that. It would only cripple her. He *was* her past and somehow she must forget him. All that mattered now was her future.

She breathed in deep and held her head high as the taxi drew up outside the airport terminal from which her flight was due to depart. This was where her future began.

It was early morning when Liana flew into Rio. The city glistened beneath a bright sun.

As the plane touched down, she felt a surge of excitement that reminded her of the way she had felt two months ago when she had flown into this very same airport for an hour and a half stop-over on her way to Buenos Aires, unaware of all the pain and upheaval that had awaited her.

But now was not then, she reminded herself swiftly as she felt a rush of memories press against her heart. Her task now was simply to do a job of work. And that was precisely what she intended doing.

She was through Immigration and Baggage Control in no time at all. Then, with her two cases piled on to a trolley, she was heading out into the arrivals hall, eyes searching beyond the barrier for a sign that would lead her to a taxi rank.

And that was probably why she failed to notice the tall dark figure in the navy linen suit until he stepped out of the crowd to stand directly in front of her.

Liana's heart slammed inside her. She longed to turn and flee. But the pounding in her brain had rendered her immobile.

Dry-mouthed, she looked up at him, into his handsome dark-eyed face, and felt her heart shrivel and die with love inside her.

Croakily, she demanded, 'What are you doing here?'

'I've come for you.' Felipe took her by the arm and firmly, with his free hand guiding the trolley, proceeded to lead her across the concourse. 'You and I, *querida*, have some talking to do.'

'No, we don't!' From somewhere, Liana found sudden strength. She pulled her arm free and tried to snatch the trolley from him. 'I'm going nowhere with you! I'm going straight to my hotel! Leave me alone! I don't want to talk to you!'

For a moment they stood there while the crowd milled around them, each with one hand on the trolley. The tall black-haired man and the slender gold-haired girl, eyes locked together, each aware of no one but the other.

Then Felipe said, 'You are not going to your hotel. You are coming back with me to El Dotado.'

Liana shook her head mutely. She felt she must be dreaming. She took a deep breath and closed her eyes tightly. When she reopened them she would discover that none of this was happening, that she wasn't standing here in the middle of Rio de Janeiro airport with Felipe telling her such strange outrageous things.

But when she opened her eyes once more nothing had altered. He was still standing there before her, his black eyes pouring through her, his expression so fierce, so intense that it made her shiver.

She said, 'You've gone crazy. Why should I do that? Why should I go with you to El Dotado?'

'Because that's where you belong.'

Liana shook her head again. What was happening? Had the whole world suddenly gone crazy?

Then Felipe spoke again. 'You belong at El Dotado.' His voice trembled with emotion. 'You belong at El Dotado, and you belong with me.'

'You *are* crazy!' It was as though the ground had fallen away beneath her. Liana scarcely dared look at him. Her heart pounded inside her. Was this his idea of a joke? 'Why are you saying these crazy things?' she demanded.

'They're not crazy, and I'm not crazy either.' With a gasp of impatience Felipe released the trolley, grasped her by both arms and held her at arm's length. 'You belong with me because you love me.'

'And who told you I loved you?' Liana felt she might faint. Suddenly everything seemed to be spinning around her.

'It doesn't matter who told me. What matters is that it's true.' He gave her a small shake. 'Go on, deny it, if you can.'

She could not. Liana let her eyes glide away, suddenly sick to her soul with shame and misery. In a small voice she implored him, 'Please let me go.'

'Never!' Again he shook her. 'Do you hear me? Never!' Then, as she gasped and blinked up at him, he pulled her roughly against him. 'I will never, all my life, let go the woman I love!'

Pressed against his chest, his arms tight around her, Liana for one moment felt that she was drowning. Confusion tore through her. Disbelief and hope and terror. If this is a dream, she prayed, please let me wake up!

But his hand was on her chin now, tilting her face to look at him, and in his eyes she could see emotions she could never have dreamed of. A mix of love and pain and desperation. Just for an instant she forgot her own anguish.

His voice a fierce whisper, Felipe demanded, 'Did you hear me? Did you hear, Liana, what I just said?'

'I heard.' Her heart was thundering inside her.

'And do you believe me? Do you believe, *querida*, that I love you—more than anything, more than my life?'

Liana gazed at him, half afraid to believe him. Yet her heart was flying on wings of happiness from her chest.

'Believe it! It's true. I love you, my darling.' With a sigh that seemed to tear his soul apart, Felipe held her for a moment hard against him, burying his face against her hair. Then, once more his eyes sought hers, his expression a torment. 'Tell me, *querida*, that you love me, too.'

Liana trembled. 'I love you.'

'And tell me that you will marry me.'

'Marry you?'

'Marry me and be with me forever. I cannot rest until I have your answer.'

Liana looked into his face, suddenly knowing beyond a doubt that this was not a dream, but a dream come true. And there, in the middle of Rio de Janeiro airport, amid the throng of human traffic that milled all about them, without a moment's hesitation, she gave him her answer.

'Yes,' she said. 'My darling Felipe, I'll marry you.'

Tonight would be her last night at El Dotado. For tomorrow Liana and Felipe would be married and then Liana would move into Felipe's house.

Barely two weeks had passed since that encounter at Rio airport, which had ended with Felipe whisking her off on the first flight back to Argentina. But not without first sweeping her into his arms and kissing her to seal the vow they had just made.

'We shall be married soon. Very soon,' he had promised her.

The remainder of that magical, breathtaking day was burned in glorious detail forever on Liana's brain.

On the three-hour flight to Buenos Aires, with Felipe holding her hand so tight that it had felt he might never release her, he had explained how he had come to be at Rio airport, so conveniently waiting for her when her flight arrived.

'It was all because of Tia Gloria's letter. The one she left for you to open on the eve of your wedding. Carreño had mentioned it to me. He wondered if you'd forgotten about it and asked my advice as to what he should do about it...'

He smiled and shook his head. 'I volunteered to deal with it. I said I'd contact you and ask you what the situation was. It was an excuse, really, I admit that. An excuse just to talk to you...' his eyes darkened '...and to find out if your marriage to Cliff was going ahead. I had to find out. I'd been thinking about nothing else, and not knowing what was going on was driving me mad.'

'Do you mean that?' The confession had delighted Liana. 'Had you really been thinking of nothing else?'

'Nothing else. Day and night.' He raised her hand to his lips and kissed her fingers. 'You are an obsession, *querida mia*. A magnificent obsession.'

He smiled as a warm flush of pleasure touched her skin. 'So yesterday I phoned you at your flat in London and some stranger answered in your place. They told me you were no longer living there and gave me another number to ring.'

'Cliff's number.' Liana nodded. 'He kindly agreed to take care of any outstanding business for me. Phone calls, mail, that kind of thing.'

'Yes, I know that now.' Felipe's hand squeezed hers hard. A fleeting look of pain touched the back of his eyes. 'But at the time I assumed that this meant you were already married. I very nearly didn't bother to call.'

Just at the thought Liana felt her heart stop. If he hadn't called, they wouldn't be here together. Their paths might never have crossed again.

'Thank heaven you did.' She whispered the words like a prayer.

'Amen to that.' Felipe's response was equally reverend. He looked into her eyes. 'But something made me do it. I still had to know for sure one way or the other.' He smiled. 'And then, of course, when I called Cliff's number, another woman's voice answered and I was totally confused.'

'Another woman? His girlfriend?' Liana smiled as Felipe nodded. She'd heard Cliff was seeing another girl these days, and she was glad for him that the romance appeared to be going well. But her eyes grew rapt with attention once more as Felipe continued his explanation.

'When she put me on to Cliff, he told me everything. About how you had broken off your engagement and were at that very moment on your way to Brazil. And then, just as I was on the point of hanging up, not quite certain what I should do next, he literally stopped me in my tracks...'

Felipe paused, his eyes searching deep into Liana's. 'He said, in that straightforward English way of his, "Of course, you know that Liana's in love with you? If you don't, I reckon it's time you did."'

Liana flushed with happy embarrassment. 'And what did you think then?'

'I didn't think at all! I knew instantly what I had to do—catch the first plane to Rio and be there to meet your flight. A team of wild horses couldn't have stopped me!'

Liana laughed, delighted. 'But I thought you hated me! You made a very good job of hiding your feelings!'

'Did I? Well, believe me, it was all an act.' He frowned. 'I know you were engaged to someone else, and I felt it my duty to respect that fact, no matter how desperately I wanted you. That was why I let you go on believing that I was your cousin and that I'd neglected Tia Gloria. I knew that would keep a distance between us.'

He paused. 'And perhaps I was a little angry with you, too. I wondered why you were marrying a man you didn't love. For I knew you didn't love Cliff. I suspected it from the beginning, and when I saw you together I knew it for certain.'

Liana had glanced away quickly, but turned to meet the dark gaze now. 'I did love Cliff, but I loved him as a friend. I was so used to having him around that I didn't even realise it myself.' Her heart squeezed inside her. Suddenly her voice was a little unsteady. 'I didn't know what real love was until I met you.'

Felipe looked into her face, his eyes dark with sensuous promise. 'All that real love is, *querida mia*, I shall teach you. When I have finished with you you will know all there is to know about love between a man and a woman.'

It had proved to be no idle promise. That very evening Liana had received the first of many lessons in the art of love.

Like a maestro of the senses he had tutored her as they lay naked together in the big double bed at El Dotado, his fingers caressing, his lips arousing, his body instructing hers in the meaning of passion.

And she was a willing pupil, eager and hungry to explore these secret realms into which she had never before strayed. Yet she could scarcely believe that her soul and her body were capable of experiencing so many exquisite pleasures. Every touch of him seemed to awaken some new delight within her.

And now, tomorrow, he would become her husband. The happiness that filled her was overwhelming.

But before they were finally joined in matrimony, there was one small thing she had to do. She had to read Great-Aunt Gloria's mysterious letter.

Felipe handed it to her now as they lay among the bedsheets, tangled and warm-scented with newly made love. He caressed her breast softly. 'Tell me what it says.'

With faintly trembling fingers, Liana ripped open the envelope and pulled out the single sheet of paper it contained. She felt a sudden anxiety, a real tug of fear that the words she was about to read might somehow have the power to jeopardise her future with Felipe.

She unfolded the sheet of paper as Felipe drew her against him, his naked body warm against her own. If anything should happen now to spoil my happiness, I shall die, Liana was thinking as she started to read.

But as her eyes scanned the first sentence, relief melted her fear.

'Just listen to this!' she told Felipe, laughing. 'It says here, "If things have worked out the way they ought, you are reading this letter on the eve of your wedding to Felipe. The fiancé you have told me about is not for you, Liana. The man for you is my beloved Felipe. I feel it in my bones. I know it in my heart. And that is why I have decided to leave half of El Dotado to each of you—so that you can squabble over it and get to know each other and finally fall in love. So, forgive an old lady for playing Cupid, and be happy together. You will be happy with no one else."'

Felipe had snatched the letter from her, his eyes wide with amazement. 'You mean the wily old bird plotted the whole thing? You mean she set this whole thing up?'

'It seems that way.' Liana's eyes were on him as, his expression incredulous, he re-read the letter. 'I hope this isn't going to change your mind about marrying me—just because you didn't think of the idea first?'

Felipe threw her a dark look that almost made her heart stop. Surely he wasn't about to demolish her by saying yes?

But he was only playing. He pulled her against him and looked into her face with eyes awash with love. 'I won't change my mind, if you promise me one thing... that you agree to name our first daughter Gloria.'

'I wouldn't dream of calling her anything else.' Liana smiled. '*First* daughter? How many are we going to have?'

Felipe kissed her face. 'As many as you want. As long as you promise me that they will all be like you.'

Liana felt her heart turn over. 'I love you,' she told him. 'I can't believe that tomorrow we'll finally be married.'

'Believe it,' he told her, his lips searching for hers. 'Married is what we're going to be for the rest of our lives.' He looked deep into her eyes. 'How does that sound?'

'It sounds like heaven,' Liana answered.

And she was right.

Next Month's Romances

Each month you can choose from a wide variety of romance with Mills & Boon. Below are the new titles to look out for next month, why not ask either Mills & Boon Reader Service or your Newsagent to reserve you a copy of the titles you want to buy — just tick the titles you would like and either post to Reader Service or take it to any Newsagent and ask them to order your books.

Please save me the following titles:	Please tick	√
DANGEROUS LOVER	Lindsay Armstrong	
RELUCTANT CAPTIVE	Helen Bianchin	
SAVAGE OBSESSION	Diana Hamilton	
TUG OF LOVE	Penny Jordan	
YESTERDAY'S AFFAIR	Sally Wentworth	
RECKLESS DECEPTION	Angela Wells	
ISLAND OF LOVE	Rosemary Hammond	
NAIVE AWAKENING	Cathy Williams	
CRUEL CONSPIRACY	Helen Brooks	
FESTIVAL SUMMER	Charlotte Lamb	
AFTER THE HONEYMOON	Alexandra Scott	
THE THREAD OF LOVE	Anne Beaumont	
SECRETS OF THE NIGHT	Joanna Mansell	
RELUCTANT SURRENDER	Jenny Cartwright	
SUMMER'S VINTAGE	Gloria Bevan	
BITES OF LOVE	Rebecca Winters	

If you would like to order these books in addition to your regular subscription from Mills & Boon Reader Service please send £1.70 per title to: Mills & Boon Reader Service, P.O. Box 236, Croydon, Surrey, CR9 3RU, quote your Subscriber No:........................ (if applicable) and complete the name and address details below. Alternatively, these books are available from many local newsagents including W.H.Smith, J.Menzies, Martins and other paperback stockists from 8th January 1993.

Name:..
Address:..
....Post Code:........................

Retailer: If you would like to stock M&B books please contact your regular book/magazine wholesaler for details.

You may be mailed with offers from other reputable companies as a result of this application. If you would rather not take advantage of these opportunities please tick box ☐

Love is in the Air...

Mills & Boon have commissioned four of your favourite authors to write four tender romances.

Guaranteed love and excitement for St. Valentine's

A BRILLIANT DISGUISE	-	Rosalie Ash
FLOATING ON AIR	-	Angela Devine
THE PROPOSAL	-	Betty Neels
VIOLETS ARE BLUE	-	Jennifer Taylor

Available from January 1993   PRICE £3

Mills & Boon

Available from Boots, Martins, John Menzies, W.H. Smith, most supermarkets and other paperback stockists. Also available from Mills & Boon Reader Service, PO Box 236, Thornton Road, Croydon, Surrey CR9 3RU.

Mills & Boon

4 FREE

Romances and 2 FREE gifts just for you!

*You can enjoy all the
heartwarming emotion of true love for FREE!
Discover the heartbreak and the happiness, the emotion and
the tenderness of the modern relationships in
Mills & Boon Romances.*

We'll send you 4 captivating Romances as a special offer from
Mills & Boon Reader Service, along with the chance to have
6 Romances delivered to your door each month.

Claim your FREE books and gifts overleaf...

An irresistible offer from Mills & Boon

Here's a personal invitation from Mills & Boon Reader Service, to become a regular reader of Romances. To welcome you, we'd like you to have 4 books, a CUDDLY TEDDY and a special MYSTERY GIFT absolutely FREE.

Then you could look forward each month to receiving 6 brand new Romances, delivered to your door, postage and packing free! Plus our free Newsletter featuring author news, competitions, special offers and much more.

This invitation comes with no strings attached. You may cancel or suspend your subscription at any time, and still keep your free books and gifts.

It's so easy. Send no money now. Simply fill in the coupon below and post it to -
Reader Service, FREEPOST, PO Box 236, Croydon, Surrey CR9 9EL.

NO STAMP REQUIRED

Free Books Coupon

Yes! Please rush me 4 free Romances and 2 free gifts! Please also reserve me a Reader Service subscription. If I decide to subscribe I can look forward to receiving 6 brand new Romances each month for just £10.20, postage and packing free. If I choose not to subscribe I shall write to you within 10 days - I can keep the books and gifts whatever I decide. I may cancel or suspend my subscription at any time. I am over 18 years of age.

Ms/Mrs/Miss/Mr_____ EP31F

Address_____

_____

Postcode_____Signature_____

Offer expires 31st May 1993. The right is reserved to refuse an application and change the terms of this offer. Readers overseas and in Eire please send for details. Southern Africa write to Book Services International Ltd, P.O. Box 42654, Craighall, Transvaal 2024. You may be mailed with offers from other reputable companies as a result of this application.
If you would prefer not to share in this opportunity, please tick box ☐